Dear Reader,

After three decades, w

Here in Australia and New Zealand, Harlequin Mills & Boon is nearly thirty years old and our range of books has kept on growing with us. So much so that it's now hard to bring you all our new titles at the start of each month - there just isn't enough room on the shelves!

So, starting this month some of your favourite series will be available at the beginning of the month and others two weeks later. You will find full details about this change on the inside front cover of this book. There, you will see which Harlequin Mills & Boon series will be available from the 1st of every month, and which series will be in-store from the 16th of every month.

This means that there'll now be exciting new books coming out every two weeks rather than every four weeks. And you will still have at least four weeks, sometimes longer, in which to buy your favourite Harlequin Mills & Boon series. And if you're one of our many readers who visits the Harlequin Mills & Boon section two or more times a month, you can now count on seeing new books there *every second week*!

Happy reading!

The Team
Harlequin Enterprises (Australia) Pty Ltd

Caroline Anderson has the mind of a butterfly. She's been a nurse, a secretary, a teacher, run her own soft-furnishing business and now she's settled on writing. She says, 'I was looking for that elusive something. I finally realised it was variety, and now I have it in abundance. Every book brings new horizons and new friends, and in between books I have learned to be a juggler. My teacher husband John and I have two beautiful and talented daughters, Sarah and Hannah, umpteen pets and several acres of Suffolk that nature tries to reclaim every time we turn our backs!' Caroline also writes for the Harlequin Mills & Boon® Medical Romance® series.

THE PREGNANT TYCOON

BY
CAROLINE ANDERSON

Harlequin
Mills & Boon

Sweet

First Published 2004
First Australian Paperback Edition 2004
ISBN 0 733 55192 0

THE PREGNANT TYCOON © 2004 by Caroline Anderson
Philippine Copyright 2004
Australian Copyright 2004
New Zealand Copyright 2004

Published by
Harlequin Mills & Boon
3 Gibbes Street
CHATSWOOD NSW 2067
AUSTRALIA

Printed and bound in Australia by
McPherson's Printing Group

CHAPTER ONE

HAPPY Birthday, Izzy. The big three-O. Terrific.

Izzy felt her smile slipping and yanked it back with effort. Any minute now her face would start to crack. For what felt like hours she'd laughed at the witty in-jokes, picked at the delicate and hideously expensive canapés and now she'd had enough. If she didn't get out of here in the next five minutes, she was going to scream.

Loudly.

It was her thirtieth birthday, and she was at a party. Not her party, though, although it was in a way her celebration. No, this was a party to celebrate the phenomenally successful flotation on the stock market of yet another company she'd rescued from certain death.

Been there, done that, she thought tiredly, but everyone was on a high, and only a real party-pooper wouldn't want to celebrate with their friends.

Friends? She gave a quiet, slightly despairing little laugh. Apart from Kate, she hadn't known any of them for more than a year at the most. Were they really friends? Or were they only there because of who and what she was?

And who was she? She knew *what* she was, and if she ever lost sight of it, the press would lose no time in reminding her with one of the selection of nicknames they thought so amusing.

The Stripper, The Assassin—Godzilla was the latest in a long line. And all because she went in where angels feared to tread, and restructured ailing companies, turning them around and pointing them in the right direction. And, of course, because she was a woman, and because she was so young, she'd attracted a lot of attention in doing it.

More, really, than was warranted. Plenty of people did what she did, but not many, she was forced to admit, with such startling results. She'd been lucky—very lucky. Her instincts had only let her down once, and the press had loved it.

But not this time. This time it had been another runaway success, and she knew she'd never need to work again.

She would, of course, simply because if she didn't work, then what would she do with her life? Without work, it was empty.

Barren.

Nonsense, she told herself. You've got a great apartment overlooking the river near Canary Wharf, a fantastic assistant in Kate, you can have anything you want—except privacy.

That was the penalty. She had more appearances in the society rags than the average royal, every date she went on was turned into a full-blown affair—which was a joke, because most men were so terrified of her they'd run screaming before they got to her bedroom door—and she was standing there surrounded by people who didn't even know her.

Heavens, *I* don't know me. Where are my real friends? Do I have any?

'Excuse me,' she murmured with a vague smile, and headed for the ladies' loo. A few minutes alone—

'You OK?'

She glanced at Kate, her right-hand-woman—and the closest thing she had to a real friend—and dredged up a smile. 'Yes, I'm fine.'

'Great party. They're a super bunch—I'll miss them. Still, there's always the next lot.'

She fell into step beside Izzy, going with her into the cloakroom, chatting to her over the top of the cubicles so even that moment of respite was denied her.

She was wondering where on earth she *could* go to be alone when Kate erupted out of the cubicle and joined her at the washbasins. 'So, how's the birthday going? I remember being thirty. Shattering. I went on the internet—that website for contacting old school-friends and so on. Found out what they were all doing. Weird.'

She chattered on, telling some involved story about a couple who'd rediscovered each other through the internet, but Izzy wasn't listening any more. Her attention had been caught by the words 'old schoolfriends', and she was miles away. Light years.

Twelve, to be exact, up in Suffolk in the long, glorious summer between leaving school and going off to uni, camping by the river in a field owned by Will's parents, all of them laughing and telling jokes and chasing each other around in the long, sweet grass, full of the joys and without a care in the world.

Where were they all now?

Rob and Emma and Julia and Sam and Lucy—and Will. Her heart lurched. Where was Will?

He'd kissed her there, down by the river in the shelter of the willows. That had been their first kiss—the first of many that blissful summer, and a prelude to more than kisses. Much, much more than kisses, she remembered with a pang of longing.

And then she'd gone to university, driven by the need to get on with her life, and he'd gone away with Julia and Rob and Emma, travelling around the world, and come back at the end of the year with news that had shattered her dreams. Her friend Julia, with whom she'd shared everything—including, apparently, Will—was pregnant with his child, and he loved her and wanted to marry her.

Her world had fallen apart that day. She'd spent the next few years reconstructing it brick by brick, until the wall she was hiding behind was so high nothing and no one could get over it. She hadn't seen him since.

Where was he now? What was he doing? Was he still with Julia? And the child—a girl or a boy? Had there been others? Little dark-haired boys and girls with his quick wit and sparkling eyes, and a smile that left her breathless...

A familiar ache of longing settled in her chest, and she dragged in a deep breath and forced her eyes to focus.

Her reflection stared back at her solemnly and did nothing to improve her humour. Mouse-brown hair, curly on a good day and like wire wool in the rain, relieved by a few delicate highlights to give it a bit of lift and stop it looking like an old pan scourer, topped a face set with dull grey-green eyes splodged with brown. A kind person would call them hazel. Her mother called them muddy. Small, even features did nothing to draw attention to her, but at least she supposed she wasn't actively ugly, and her smile, when she could be bothered to produce it, was OK.

She practised it fleetingly, and scowled. OK? Just barely.

'All done?'

Her eyes swung across to meet Kate's in the mirror and she summoned that elusive and barely OK smile. 'Yes, I'm all done. Let's go back to the party.'

Steve was waiting for her—suave, sophisticated, and relentless—and for some reason totally unable to light her fire.

Not that he was alone. Nothing and no one seemed to light her fire these days, either personally or professionally. She'd lost interest in everything, and she was filled with a strange restlessness that made her snappy and short-tempered.

'I thought you'd deserted me, Isabella,' he said with a smile that made her skin crawl.

She gave a brief, humourless laugh. 'No such luck,' she said, and he gave her a rather peculiar look, as if he couldn't quite work out if it was an insult or not. Her head was starting to ache, and she knew it would be at least another two hours before she could get out of there.

'Are you OK, Bella?' he asked her, apparently genuine concern showing now on his smooth, rather characterless face. He was probably just looking for an excuse to take her home, she reasoned, but repelling his advances yet again was absolutely the last thing she needed. Knowing her luck there'd be a photographer lurking, anyway, and she didn't believe in the old maxim that there was no such thing as bad publicity.

There was, and she'd had enough of it to last her a lifetime. A single glimpse of her on the arm of the very recently divorced CEO would be enough to put another notch on the imaginary bedpost that the gutter press had dreamed up out of thin air, and there was no way she was adding any more fuel to that particular fire.

'Just a bit of a headache,' she said, digging out *that smile* again. 'I'll be fine—and don't call me Bella. You know it's not my name.'

He laughed, quite unmoved by her reprimand. He seemed unmoved by most things, she thought, and not for the first time she wondered what made him tick. Money, probably—lots of it, and preferably somebody else's. Still, he wouldn't need to worry about that now, not since her makeover of his company. She'd made him rich beyond his wildest dreams, and women would be all over him like flies on a muck heap.

He trailed a finger up her bare arm, pausing thoughtfully at her shoulder before slipping his fingertip under her strap and toying with it absently. 'We ought to get together, you know, Isabel,' he murmured, getting her name right for once. 'How about Friday evening? We could do dinner—somewhere quiet.'

'Quiet sounds good,' Izzy muttered under her breath, not really referring to his suggestion, but he pounced on it like a terrier with a rat, and she couldn't be bothered to argue. Before she could draw breath he'd arranged the venue, the time and told her what to wear. If she hadn't had such a headache coming on, she would have told him what he could do with his quiet night. As it was she just stifled a sigh and nodded.

She persevered until midnight, then, excusing herself, she took a taxi home and let herself into her cool, tranquil apartment with a sigh of relief. *This* was quiet. This was what she needed.

She heeled off her shoes, padded over to the kitchen and filled a glass with iced water from the cooler in the fridge door, then dropped gratefully into the corner of the comfortable sofa, her feet tucked up underneath her on the butter-soft leather as she stared blindly out over the city skyline.

Lights twinkled, millions of them. All those people out there busily getting on with their lives, she thought, the clubs and bars in this thriving corner of the capital throbbing with life. It was still early by their standards, merely the beginning of the night. Even the thought exhausted her.

She rubbed her temples, pulling out the pins that held her unwilling hair in place. It sprang free, a wild tangle of curls tumbling down over her shoulders, and instantly her headache eased. She sighed and dropped her head back against the soft cushion of the sofa and closed her eyes.

She wanted to open the window, to slide back the big glass pane and step out onto the roof garden, but all she would hear would be the honking traffic and the sirens, the sounds of the city by night.

It would be quiet in the country, she thought, the only sounds the rustlings and cries of the animals. Perhaps quiet wasn't the word. She thought again of their campsite by the river all those years ago, the astonishing sounds of the countryside at night, and she had a fierce longing to return, to hear the sounds again.

Kate's words came back to her, piquing her curiosity, and she got up and went over to her computer.

With a few keystrokes she connected to the internet, and within minutes she'd registered with the website Kate had talked about and was scanning a list of once-familiar names.

Rob's name sprang out, and she clicked on the envelope beside it to read his message. It was so much like him that she could almost hear his voice. He was a solicitor now, married to Emma, they had three children, and they still lived in the village.

How incredible, after all this time, that they were still there in the same place. She felt a little stab of something that could have been envy, but crushed it ruthlessly. What was she thinking about? She had a fantastic life—success, wealth beyond her wildest expectations, a full and hectic schedule.

What more could she possibly want?

Will.

She ignored the curiously painful thought, dismissing it before it took hold. She'd e-mail Rob, and ask him how everyone was. Without stopping to think too much, she wrote a quick e-mail and then as an afterthought included her telephone number.

Maybe he'd ring and they could have a chat.

'Michael, I'm not telling you again, do your homework or that GameBoy's going in the bin. Rebecca? Beccy, where are you? Your stuff's scattered about all over the place.'

She wandered in, her mouth formed in a sulky pout around her thumb, and with ill grace she shovelled her books back into her school bag and flounced off again.

Will sighed and rammed a hand through his hair. He had the accounts to do, another endless round of forms to fill in for yet another set of regulations—and when he'd finished that, he'd have the ewes to check—again. Still, at least it was warm now. Lambing in April, even if it was by accident, knocked spots off lambing in February.

The phone rang, freeing him from the paperwork he hated, and he scooped up the receiver almost gratefully.

'Hello, Valley Farm.'

'Will—it's Rob. Just making sure that you haven't forgotten the party.'

His heart sank, the gratitude evaporating. 'No, I haven't forgotten,' he lied. 'When is it?'

'Friday—seven-thirty onwards, at the house. You are coming, aren't you? Emma will give me such hell if you don't.'

And him too, no doubt. 'I'll try,' he promised evasively. 'I might be able to get away for an hour or so, but I'm still lambing, so don't rely on me.' He didn't need anyone else relying on him. He felt as if the weight of the world was on his shoulders as it was, and the party was just one more thing he had to do out of duty.

'Stuff the lambs.'

'With garlic and rosemary?'

'Smartass. Just be there,' Rob said firmly, and the dial tone sounded in his ear.

He dropped the receiver back into the cradle and

scowled at it. If it was anybody else, any way on God's earth he could get out of it, he'd do exactly that. He couldn't, though. It was Rob and Emma, their tenth wedding anniversary and thirtieth birthday joint celebration, and he had no choice.

That didn't mean, however, that he had to enjoy it or stay longer than was strictly necessary!

Two hours, tops, he promised himself. And duty done, honour satisfied, he'd be able to come home and—

And what? Sit here in the empty house on his own and stare morosely at the four walls? Go alone to his big, empty bed and lie staring at the ceiling, equally morosely, until sleep claimed him?

He snorted. He could always tackle some of the endless paperwork that dogged his life and drove him to distraction. God knows, there was enough of it.

Shooting back his chair, he went through to the kitchen, noting almost absently that Michael was now doing his homework, albeit in front of the television, and Rebecca was curled in the big chair with the dog squeezed up beside her and a cat on her lap, her eyes wilting.

'I'm just going outside to check the sheep,' he told them, hooking his elderly jacket off the back of the door and stuffing his feet into his muddy Wellington boots. 'Beccy, bed in twenty minutes. Michael, you've got one hour.'

He went out into the cold, quiet night and made his way across to the barns. There were warm sleepy noises coming from the animals, soft bleats and shufflings in the straw, and he could hear the horses moving on the other side of the partition that divided the barn.

He did a quick check of the lambs, made sure none of the ewes was in trouble, then, satisfied that all was quiet, he cast an eye over the other stock: the chickens and ducks all shut up for the night, the house cow and the few beef calves out in the pasture behind the house. Then he checked the horses that were not his but were there on a DIY livery. He always included them in his late-night check, just to be sure they had water and none of them had rolled and got themselves cast, stuck firmly up against the side wall and unable to stand up again.

All was well, though, and with his arms folded on the top of the gate he paused for a moment, drinking in the quiet night.

A fox called, and in the distance he could hear a dog barking. Owls hooted to each other, and the pale, ghostly shape of a barn owl drifted past on the night air, on the lookout for an unwary mouse.

Vaulting over the gate, he left the stockyard and walked round to the old farmyard on the other side of the house, looking round at all the changes that had been made in the last few years.

The old timber cowshed and feed store had been turned into a thriving farm shop and café, selling a range of wonderful mainly organic foods, many of them cooked by his mother. She ran that side of the enterprise, while his father supervised the timber side of the business, the garden furniture and wooden toys and willow fencing which were now manufactured on-site in the old milking parlour.

Diversify, they'd been told, and so they had. Instead of boggy, indifferent grazing down by the river, only usable in the height of the summer, they now grew coppiced willow, cutting it down to the ground every winter and harvesting the supple young shoots while they were dormant. They were used to make environmentally friendly and renewable screens and hurdle-style fencing panels, now hugely popular, and all sorts of other things, many to special order.

He still grew crops on the majority of the farm, of course, but it was going organic, a long process full of bureaucracy and hoops of red tape that he had to jump through in order to satisfy the stringent requirements of the food industry, and then there were the sheep. In a few weeks, when the lambs were a bit tougher, he'd move them down to the saltmarsh pasture on the old Jenks' farm, because organic saltmarsh lamb fetched a huge premium in the specialist restaurant market.

Buying up the farm from Mrs Jenks had been a major investment at a time when they couldn't really afford it, but it had been a one-off opportunity and there had been no choice. It had spread their resources even further, however, and made more work, and it would be years before they got a return.

Small wonder, he thought, that he was tired all the time. Still, the farm was thriving again, their futures were secure, and that was all he asked.

With one last glance round to make sure that nothing had been overlooked, he went back inside. There was a little scurry and he saw the tail-end of his daughter disappearing through the doorway. He suppressed a smile and laid a friendly hand on Michael's shoulder.

'How're you doing, sport?'

'OK, I suppose. Just got my French to do now.'

Will chuckled ruefully. 'Not my strong point, I'm afraid. You'll have to ask your grandmother if you get stuck.'

He put the kettle on, and went upstairs to check on Rebecca. She was already in bed, with very little sign of having washed her face or cleaned her teeth, and he chivvied her through the bathroom and then tucked her up in bed.

'Read me a story,' she pleaded, and although he was exhausted, he picked up the book from beside her bed, settled down next to her with his back propped against the headboard and his arm around her shoulders, and started to read.

'Dad?'

Will sucked in a deep breath and forced his eyes open. 'Michael? What time is it?'

'Nearly ten. You've been here for ages.'

Will glanced down at Rebecca, snuggled against his chest fast asleep, and gently eased his arm out from behind her and settled her down onto the pillow. 'Sorry,' he murmured, getting to his feet. 'I just sat down to read her a story—I must have dropped off.'

'You look knackered,' his son said, eyeing him worriedly. 'You work too hard these days.'

Will ruffled his hair affectionately and gave him a brief hug. 'I'll live,' he said, and wondered if it was only to his own ears that it sounded like a vow.

'Good grief. Emma?' Rob pushed his chair back from the computer and turned towards the study door as his wife came in.

She propped herself against the doorframe, arms folded across her chest, and tipped her head on one side. 'What is it?' she asked him. 'You look as if you've seen a ghost.'

He gave a shaky chuckle. 'Well—in a way. It's Isabel Brooke. She's sent me an e-mail. She wants to get in touch. I've got her phone number—shall we ring her?'

Emma shrugged away from the doorframe and came and stood beside him, her hand on his shoulder, peering at the screen. 'Well. Wow—the famous Isabel Brooke! You could always ask her to the party.'

Rob gave a startled cough of laughter. 'You have to be joking! Why on earth would she want to come up here to our boring, pedestrian, provincial party?'

Emma slapped him lightly on the shoulder. 'Hey! This is *our* party. It's going to be the best party this county has seen in a long while. Boring and provincial, my foot. Anyway, she might like it.'

Rob chuckled again. 'I stand by to be amazed. So, shall I ask her?'

Emma shrugged slightly. 'Why not? She'll either say yes or no.'

'Sometimes, my darling, you are so profound.' Rob stood and wrapped his arms around his wife. 'It's too late tonight. I'll ring her tomorrow. Just now, I have better things to do…'

'Isabel? There's a call for you—somebody called Rob. I told him you were in a meeting, but he said it couldn't wait.'

Kate was hovering, her head stuck round the meeting room door, waiting for her answer. Izzy frowned and rubbed the little crease between her brows with a small, blunt fingertip. 'Kate, I really don't have time for—' She hesitated, a thought occurring to her. 'Did he give a surname?'

Kate shook her head. 'He just said you go way back.'

Izzy smiled apologetically at the people gathered around the table. 'Would you excuse me?' she murmured. 'I won't be a moment. Kate, could you be a love and see if anyone needs more coffee?'

She went out into her office and picked up the phone. 'Isabel Brooke,' she said, curiosity vying with wariness.

'I was beginning to think you weren't serious about getting back in touch with us—or were you just making me cool my heels so I know my place?' the familiar voice said laughingly, and Izzy felt her mouth kick up in a smile.

'And hello yourself,' she said, settling down in her chair with her feet propped on the edge of her desk, crossed at the ankles. A smile played at the corners of her mouth. She picked a little bit of fluff off her trousers and smoothed the fabric absently. 'I'm sorry, I really was in a meeting, and I'd said no calls. I didn't realise I'd given you my office number.'

'You didn't, but I didn't want to leave it too late, so I got my secretary to do a bit of sleuthing. How are you?'

'I'm fine. Great. How are you? And Emma? Three kids now! I'm impressed.'

He laughed. 'Don't be. They were the easy bit. We're all fine—really good, but nothing like as spectacular as you! Talk about a meteoric rise in the world.'

Izzy shrugged, then realised he couldn't see her. 'It's only money,' she said dismissively, realising that it was true. What was her success when measured against Rob and Emma's happiness and the birth of their three children? She swallowed a lump of what had to be self-pity, and put her feet back on the floor.

'Look, Rob, I really am rather tied up this morning, but I'd love to see you all. Is there any way we can meet up?'

'Actually, that's why I'm phoning you. Emma and I are having a party to celebrate our tenth wedding anniversary and our thirtieth birthdays, and we want you to come. The trouble is, it's tomorrow night. Not very much notice, I'm afraid, and I expect you're so busy you won't be able to make it, but loads of us will be there and it would be really great to see you.'

Something big and awkward was swelling in her chest, making it hard for her to breathe, and there was a silly smile plastered to her face that she couldn't seem to shift.

'That would be fantastic. Of course I'll come—I wouldn't miss it for the world. I'll hand you back to my secretary and you can give her all the details, and I'll see you on Friday. Thanks, Rob.'

She spoke briefly to Kate and asked her to get all the relevant information from Rob and book her a hotel room nearby, and then, ruthlessly suppressing a twinge of guilt, she also asked her to contact Steve and cancel the dinner engagement he'd talked her into at her party. Then, forcing herself to concentrate, she went back into the meeting and smiled brightly at the assembled company.

'Sorry about that, everybody. Now, where were we?'

Izzy was a mass of nerves. It was quite ridiculous. She did very much more scary things than this every day of her life, and yet, for some reason, this whole event had taken on the most enormous significance.

Because of Will? What if he was there? And Julia? Oh, Lord.

She checked the address and eyed the house warily, reluctant to go in there yet. Twelve years was a long time, and a lot had happened. Too much? They always said you should never go back, but maybe it was time. Maybe this was just what she needed to get closure.

She checked her appearance one last time in the little rearview mirror of her car, and then with a mental shrug she abandoned any further prevarication, got out of the car and strode purposefully towards the open front door, the flowers she'd brought clutched just a little tightly in her hand.

As she drew nearer she could hear the sounds of a party in full swing—loud voices, shouts of laughter, the insistent rhythm of music that invaded her blood. It would be pointless to ring the doorbell, she realised, and so, her heart pounding in time to the beat, she walked down the hall and through the open door at the end, a smile plastered to her face.

For a moment no one noticed her, then a sudden

silence fell, and everyone seemed to turn towards her. Her smile was slipping, brittle, and she stared at the room full of strangers and wondered what on earth she was doing there.

Then a man detached himself from the crowd, shorter than she remembered, his body more solid, his hair thinner, but the sparkling green eyes and the smile that encompassed the world were just the same, and he strode towards her, arms outstretched.

'Izzy!'

'Rob,' she said with relief, and went into his arms with a sense of homecoming that took her by surprise.

He released her, holding her at arm's length and studying her, then dragging her back into his arms for another bear hug. 'Emma!' he called. 'Look who it is!'

Emma hadn't changed at all. She was still the friendly, lovely girl she'd always been, and she hugged Izzy, took the flowers with an exclamation of delight and dragged her off to meet all the others.

Well, most of them. There was no sign of Will, and Izzy suppressed the strange sense of disappointment that prickled at her. She'd had no reason to suppose he would be there, so it was ludicrous to feel so bereft at his absence.

Anyway, if he'd been there, Julia would have been, as well, and she wasn't sure that she was ready to meet her again, even all those years later.

And then there was another sudden silence, and her eyes were drawn to the doorway.

A man filled it, his dark hair untidy and rumpled as if he'd just combed it with his fingers, although they were now rammed firmly in his pockets. He looked awkward and uncomfortable, ready for flight, but before he had the chance to make his escape the spell broke and the crowd surged round him, wrapping him in a welcome as warm as it was inescapable.

And then he looked up across the crowded room and met her eyes, and her heart jammed in her throat.

Dear God, after all these years. He hasn't changed, she thought, then shook her head slowly. No, he has changed, but he's still—Will. My Will.

No.

Yes!

Stop it. Never mind that. Look at him. Look at the changes. He's bigger—taller, heavier, older. His eyes look tired. Beautiful, still staggeringly beautiful, but tired.

Why so tired?

She wanted to cry, to laugh, to hug him—and because she could do none of them, she retreated, through a door she found conveniently placed behind her, and fled into the sanctuary of another hallway.

She needed time—time to think. Time to get her ducks in a row and her heart back under control before she said or did something stupid.

Oh, Lord. Will…

CHAPTER TWO

WILL was stunned. He wouldn't have imagined in a million years that Izzy would be here. Of all the places, all the ways he'd imagined meeting her again, this hadn't even been on the list. Somebody was pressing a drink into his hand, somebody else was slapping him on the back, saying how good it was to see him again, but all he could think about was Izzy.

His Izzy.

No. Not now. Not any more. Not for years—not since he'd betrayed her trust—

Hell, why hadn't Rob warned him? Would he still have come?

Fool. Of course he would have come. Wild horses wouldn't have kept him away. He needed to speak to her, but first he had to greet all these people who were so pleased to see him—good people who'd supported them through the nightmare of the last few years. So he smiled and laughed and made what he hoped were sensible remarks, and when he looked up again, she was gone.

Inexplicably, panic filled him. 'Excuse me,' he muttered, and, squeezing his way through the crowd, he went through the doorway at the back of the room that led out to the side hall. It had been the door nearest to her, and the most likely one for her to have used to make her escape, but he couldn't let her go until he'd

24

spoken to her. He was suddenly afraid that she would have slipped out and gone away, that he wouldn't have a chance to speak to her, and he had to speak to her.

There was so much to say—

She hadn't gone anywhere. She was standing in the side hall looking lost, absently shredding a leaf on the plant beside her, her fabled composure scattered to the four winds. The powerful, dynamic woman of the glossy society magazines was nowhere to be seen, and in her face was an extraordinary and humbling vulnerability. His panic evaporated.

'Hello, Izzy,' he said softly. 'Long time no see.'

Her smile wavered and then firmed with a visible effort. 'Hello, Will,' she replied, and her voice was just as warm and mellow and gentle as he'd remembered. 'How are you?'

'Oh, you know,' he said with a wry smile. 'Still farming.' He ran his eyes over her elegant and sophisticated evening trousers and pretty little spangled top, and his gut tightened. 'You're looking as beautiful as ever—not the least bit like an assassin.'

'Still the old sweet talker, then,' she murmured, her lips kicking up in a smile that nearly took his legs out from under him. 'Anyway, I'm surprised you remember. It's been a long time—twelve years.'

'Eleven since I saw you last—but I've got the newspapers and the glossies to remind me, lest I should forget,' he told her, trying to keep his voice light and his hands to himself.

She rolled her eyes expressively, and a chuckle managed to find its way out of the constricted remains of his throat.

'So—how's Julia?' she asked, and he felt his smile fade. Oh, hell. There was no easy way to do this.

'She's dead, Izzy,' he said gently. 'She's been dead a little over two years. She had cancer.'

Even though his words were softly spoken, he felt their impact on her like a physical blow. Her eyes widened, her mouth opening in a little cry as her hand flew up to cover it. 'Will, no—I'm so sorry. I had no idea. Oh, Will—'

If he'd had any sense he would have kept his distance, but he couldn't. She looked so forlorn, so grief-stricken. He took one step towards her, and she covered the ground between them so fast he barely had time to open his arms. She hit his chest with a thud, her arms wrapping tightly round him in a gesture of comfort that was so typically Izzy it took his breath away.

Dear God, he thought wildly. She felt the same—she even smelt the same. It was almost as if the last twelve years had never happened—his marriage to Julia, the two children, her slow, lingering death, the long fight back to normality—all that swept away with just one touch.

Her body trembled in his arms, and he tightened them reflexively around her. 'Shh—it's all right,' he murmured softly, and gradually her trembling body steadied and she eased away from him. Reluctantly, yet knowing it was common sense, he let her go and stepped back.

Her hand came up and caught a tendril of hair, tucking it back behind her ear, and her smile was sad. 'I'm sorry. I really had no idea, Will. It must have been dreadful for you all. Why didn't Rob tell me? I can't believe it—I'm so sorry I brought it up like that, spoiling the party.'

He laughed, a rough, scratchy sound even to his ears, and met her anguished eyes with a smile. 'You haven't spoilt the party. I hate parties anyway, and besides, mentioning Julia doesn't change anything. We talk about her all the time. Her death is just a fact of life.'

He wanted to talk to her, to share the huge number of things that had happened for both of them in that time, but people were coming through the hall, heading for the cloakroom or the kitchen, and they all paused for a chat.

He felt the evening ebbing away, and panic rose again in his chest. He couldn't let her go again without talking to her, properly, without constant interruptions. There was so much to say—too much, and most of it best left unsaid, but still—

'Look, it would be really nice to catch up with you— I don't suppose you've got any time tomorrow, have you?' he suggested, wondering as he said the words whether he himself could find any time in the middle of what was bound to be a ridiculously hectic schedule.

'I'm staying at the White Hart for the night,' she said. 'I was going to head back some time tomorrow, but I don't have any definite plans. What did you have in mind?'

He crossed his fingers behind his back and hoped his father could help out with the children. 'Come for lunch,' he suggested. 'You'll know how to find the farmhouse—it hasn't moved.'

His smile was wry, and she answered with a soft laugh. 'That would be lovely. I'll look forward to it.'

They fell silent, the sounds of the party scarcely able to intrude on the tension between them, but then the door opened behind him yet again and Rob came out, punching him lightly on the arm.

'Here you both are! Come and circulate—you can't hog each other, it's not on. Everyone wants to talk to you both.'

And without ceremony he dragged them back into the party and forced them to mingle. They were separated from each other within moments, and when Will's phone rang to call him back to a difficult lambing, she was nowhere to be found. Still, he'd see her in the morning.

He shrugged his coat on, said goodbye to Rob and Emma and went back to the farm. It was only later, as he crawled into bed at three o'clock with the lambs safely delivered, that he realised they hadn't discussed a time.

Izzy pulled up outside the farmhouse and stared around her in astonishment.

Well, it was certainly different! The house looked pretty much the same, and the barns behind it, but beyond the mellow old brick wall dividing the house from the other side of the farmyard there had been some huge changes.

The weatherboarding on the old farm buildings was all new and freshly stained black, sharp against the soft red of the tiled roofs, and on the front of one was a sign saying, 'The Old Crock's Café'. There was a low fence around an area of tables and chairs, and though it was still only April, there were people sitting outside enjoying the glorious sunshine.

There were other changes, too, beyond the café. The farm shop beside it seemed to be doing a brisk trade, and on the other side of what was now a car park the big building that she was sure had once been the milking parlour now housed an enterprise called Valley Timber Products. She could see chunky wooden playground toys and what looked like garden furniture in a small lawned area beside it.

There was a basket shop, as well, selling all sorts of things like willow wreaths and planters and wigwams for runner beans, as well as the more traditional baskets, and she could see that, at a quarter to eleven on a Saturday morning, the whole place was buzzing.

A thriving cottage industry, she thought, and wondered who ran all the various bits and pieces of this little complex and how much of it was down to Will. He probably let all the units to enterprising individuals, she reasoned. There wouldn't be enough hours in the day to do anything else.

She turned back to the house, conscious of the fact that it was still not eleven o'clock and she was probably rather early for lunch, but she'd been asked to vacate her room by ten, and after driving somewhat aimlessly around for half an hour, she'd decided to get it over with and come straight here.

Get it over with, she thought. *Like going to the dentist.* How strange, to be so nervous with Will, of all people, but her heart was pounding and her palms were damp and she hadn't been so edgy since she'd held her first board meeting.

At least then she'd had an agenda. Now she was meeting the widowed husband of her old schoolfriend, father of the child whose conception had been the kiss of death for their relationship.

Bizarre.

'If you're looking for Will, he's in with the lambs,' a woman called, pointing round the back of the house, and with a smile of thanks, she headed round towards the barns.

'Will?' she called. 'Are you there?'

A dog came running up, a black and white collie, grinning from ear to ear and wagging at her hopefully, then it ran back again, hopping over a gate and heading into a barn.

She eyed the mud thoughtfully, glanced down at her Gucci boots with regret and picked her way over to the gate.

'Will?'

'In here,' a disembodied voice yelled, and she wrestled with the gate—why did farm gates never swing true on their hinges?—and went through into the barn. It took her eyes a moment to adjust, and when they had, she spotted him crouched down on the far side of the little barn with a sheep. It was bleating pitifully, and as she picked her way across the straw bedding, Will grunted and glanced up, then rolled his eyes and gave a wry smile.

'Hi,' he said softly. 'Sorry, didn't realise it was you. Welcome to the mad house. You're early.'

'I know. I'm sorry—do you want me to go away?'

He shook his head. 'No. Can you give me a minute? I'm a little tied up.'

She suddenly realised what he was doing, and for a moment considered escaping back to the café to give him time to finish, but then the ewe tried to struggle to her feet, and with his other hand—the one that wasn't buried up to the elbow in her back end—he grabbed her and wrestled her back down to the straw.

'Anything I can do to help?' she found herself asking, and he gave her a slightly incredulous look and ran his eyes over her assessingly.

'If you really mean that, you could kneel on her neck,' he said, and she could tell he expected her to turn tail.

She did, too, but then, to her own amazement as much as his, she gave a little shrug, dropped her Louis Vuitton bag into the soiled straw and knelt down in her Versace jeans and Gucci boots and put her knee gently on the ewe's neck.

'By the way, good morning,' she said, and smiled.

Will was stunned.

If the paparazzi who hounded her for the glossy society mags could see her now, he thought with an inward chuckle, they'd never believe it.

'Morning,' he said, and then grunted with pain as the ewe contracted down on his hand and crushed a sharp little hoof into his fingers. Well, at least he knew where one leg was, he thought philosophically, and the moment the contraction eased, he grabbed the offending hoof, traced it up to the shoulder, found the other leg, tugged them both straight and then persuaded the little nose to follow suit.

Moments later, with another heave from Mum and a

firm, solid tug from Will, twin number one was born, followed moments later by the second.

And the third.

'Triplets?' she said, her voice soft and awed, and he shot her a grin and sat back on his heels, using a handful of straw to scrub at the soggy little morsels with their tight yellow perms and wriggling tails.

'Apparently so.' They struggled to their feet, knees wobbling, and made their way to their mother, on her feet by now, and Will got up and looked ruefully at his hands.

'I'd help you up, but—'

She grinned up at him, her soft green eyes alight with joy, and his heart lurched, taking him by surprise. She stood easily, brushing down her knees with a careless hand. 'That was wonderful,' she said, the joy showing in her voice as well as her eyes, and he wanted to hug her.

Instead he took a step back, gathered up his bucket of hot water and soap and towel, and quickly made a pen around the little family.

'We'll leave them to it. They've got all they need for now.'

'Why isn't that one feeding?' Izzy asked, staring worriedly at the lambs as one of them stood by bleating forlornly and butting its mother without success.

'They've only got two teats, but she's had triplets before. They'll take turns and she'll sort them out. She's a good mother. Come, Banjo.'

He ushered her towards the back door, the dog at his heels, and, kicking the door shut behind them, he stripped off his padded shirt and scrubbed his arms in the sink.

'Don't mind me,' she said dryly, and he looked up, suddenly self-conscious, to find her laughing softly at him across the kitchen.

He felt his mouth quirk into a grin, and he shook his head. 'Sorry. Didn't think. Actually, I could do with a shower. Can you give me five minutes?'

'Of course.'

'Make yourself at home,' he told her, and then, as he ran up the stairs, he remembered the photos of Julia and the children all over the piano in the corner.

He shrugged. What could he do? She'd been his wife, the mother of his children. She deserved to be remembered, and he couldn't protect Izzy from that reality any more than he could have prevented Julia's death.

She looked around the kitchen, so much as it had been all those years ago, and felt as if she was caught in a time warp.

Any minute now Rob and Emma and Julia, and maybe Sam or Lucy, would come through that door from the farmyard, laughing and chattering like magpies, and Mrs Thompson would put the kettle on the hob and pull a tray of buns out of the oven.

She'd always been baking, the kitchen heady with the scent of golden Madeira cake and fragrant apple pies and soft, floury rolls still hot in the middle. She'd fed everybody who came over her threshold, Izzy remembered, and nobody was ever made to feel unwelcome.

And at Christmas they'd always come here carol-singing last, and gather round the piano to sing carols and eat mince pies hot from the oven.

With a tender, reminiscent smile still on her lips, Izzy turned towards the piano—and stopped dead, her heart crashing against her ribs. Slowly, as if she had no right to be there but couldn't help herself, she crossed the room on reluctant feet and stood there, rooted to the spot, studying the pictures.

Julia and Will, laughing together on the swing under the apple tree. Julia with a baby in her arms and a toddler leaning against her knee. Will on the swing again, with the toddler on his lap, laughing, and another one with the baby, nose to nose, his expression so tender it brought tears to her eyes.

What am I doing here? I don't belong! This is her house—her husband.

She turned, stumbling blindly towards the door, and Will caught her and folded her into his arms, cradling her against his chest as the sobs fought free and racked her body.

'Shh. I'm sorry. I should have realised it would upset you. I'd forgotten how much you loved her.'

Loved you, Izzy corrected silently, but she couldn't speak, and anyway, it didn't seem like the smartest thing to say under the circumstances.

Her sobs faded as quickly as they'd come, the shock of her reaction receding in the security of his arms, and gently he released her and stood back, looking down at her with worried eyes.

'OK now?'

She nodded, scrubbing her nose with the back of her

hands, and he passed her a handful of kitchen roll and waited while she blew her nose and mopped her eyes and dragged out that smile.

'Sorry,' she mumbled. 'Too many memories.'

He nodded and turned away, his face tight, and she could have kicked herself. If she had too many memories, what on earth did he have?

'Tea?'

'Please.'

He put the kettle on, then turned and propped himself against the front rail of the Aga and studied her thoughtfully. Uncomfortable with his scrutiny, she studied him back and fired off the first salvo.

'You've changed,' she said, her voice almost accusing.

He snorted softly. 'I should hope so. I was a puny kid of nineteen the last time you saw me. I've grown two, maybe three inches and put on a couple of stone. I work hard—physical stuff. That builds muscle.'

It did, and she'd seen the evidence for herself just a few moments ago when he'd stripped off at the sink. Putting the disturbing memory away, she shook her head, studying the lines on his face, the lingering trace of sadness in his eyes. 'I didn't mean that,' she said, and then gave a short, hollow laugh. 'I'm sorry, I'm being a real idiot here. Of course you've changed, after all you've been through. Who wouldn't?'

His smile was wry. 'Who indeed? Still—it's all over now, and we're moving on.' He cocked his head on one side and his smile softened. 'You don't look any different,' he said, his voice a trifle gruff, and she rolled her eyes.

'All that money, all that sophistication, and I don't look any different?' She'd meant to sound a light note, but instead she sounded like a petulant little toddler. How silly, to feel hurt. After all, she probably hadn't changed that much. Nothing had touched her as it had touched him.

Not since he'd gone away.

But Will was looking embarrassed, and she wanted to kick herself again. He scrubbed a hand through his hair and gave an impatient sigh. 'I meant—oh, hell, I don't know what I meant, except it wasn't an insult— or not intended to be. I'm sorry if it came over like that.'

His eyes were full of remorse, and she shook her head and reached out, laying a gentle hand on his arm. 'Of course it didn't. I just feel different, and I suppose I thought it might be reflected in my face, but a sensible woman would be flattered. Anyway, I wouldn't want my money to have changed me, and I certainly don't want to look like Godzilla, so perhaps I should just be grateful!'

His mouth lifted in a wry smile, and his eyes swept her face, their expression tender. 'I suppose you have changed, a little, but you're still you, every bit as beautiful as you ever were, and it's really good to see you again. That's what I was trying to say in my clumsy, inept way.'

She laughed, her turn now to be embarrassed, and shook her head. 'I'm not beautiful—'

'I'm not going to argue with you,' he said, but his thumb came up and brushed away the last remnant of her tears, and the tender gesture nearly brought her to her knees. Then he dropped his hand and stepped away, ramming it into his pocket, turning away.

When he spoke, his voice was gruff. 'It's a bit of a shock, really, seeing you again—takes me back all those years. But that's never a good idea, and you can't really go back, can you? Too much water under too many bridges.'

And just then some of that water came pouring into the kitchen in the form of a tidal wave of giggling and chasing and high-pitched shrieks that skidded to a halt the moment they saw her.

The little girl she was ready for—dark-haired, blue-eyed, the image of her father. The boy, though—he stopped her in her tracks. His colouring was almost the same, but it was the shape of his face, the expression, the vulnerable tilt to his mouth.

Julia.

Will straightened up, looking down at them with pride in his eyes.

'Izzy, meet my children—Michael and Rebecca. Kids, this is Isabel. She was at school with me and your mother. Say hi.'

'Hi,' they chorused, and then their four eyes swivelled back to him and mischief sparkled in them again. 'Grannie says can we ask you for some more eggs, because everybody wants egg sandwiches today and she's run out,' Rebecca said in a rush.

'And Grandad's sold a climbing frame and a tree house this morning, and you know old Mrs Jenks?' Michael said, his eyes alight. 'She's having a willow coffin. She's going to have a woodland burial, and her son's up in arms. I heard Grannie telling Grandad.

They were arguing about it in the café, and she said it was her body, she could do what she wanted with it. And Grannie said to tell you there's roast pepper flan today,' Michael added inconsequentially, and Izzy felt her lips twitch.

Will was smiling at them, ruffling Michael's hair and slinging a casual, affectionate arm around his daughter's shoulders, and Izzy felt suddenly empty.

I've got nothing. Thirty years, and I've got nothing. Nothing to hand on except money, and no one even to give that to. No wonder I haven't changed.

The kettle boiled, its shrill whistle fracturing the moment and freeing her.

'I'll make the tea—you get the eggs,' she said, and opened the cupboard the mugs had always lived in.

'Try the dishwasher,' he said over his shoulder as they went out, and she pulled down its door and found mugs—lots of mugs, unwashed, even though the machine was full. She put powder in the dispenser, shut the door and set it going, then washed the two mugs she'd rescued and made the tea, lifting out the teabags just as he came back in.

'Find everything?'

'Just about. I put the dishwasher on.'

'Oh, damn,' he said. 'I meant to do that.' His grin was wry. 'I meant to do all sorts of things, but you were early and the ewe was late, and—' He broke off, the grin widening as he shrugged, and then he sighed and wrapped his arms around her again, and hugged her briefly against that wonderfully solid chest that she had no rights to.

'It really is good to see you again,' he murmured,

releasing her to look down searchingly into her eyes. 'Are you OK? Really OK?'

She found that smile somehow, and the lie to go with it. 'I'm fine. How about you? You've had so much more to contend with.'

His eyes tracked away, then back, and his smile was fleeting. 'Yes. I'm OK now. It's been a rough few years.'

'Tell me,' she said softly, and he picked up his mug and pulled out a chair for her, then sat in the carver at the head of the table, his father's chair if she remembered right, and stared down into his tea.

'It was nearly three years ago. She'd been having difficulty swallowing, and she felt as if there was something stuck in her throat, so she went to the doctor. He referred her to the hospital, and they diagnosed cancer of the oesophagus. She had treatment, but it was only to make it less uncomfortable for her. We knew that right from the beginning. She reckoned it was because of the chemicals in our food, and she'd had concerns about that for some time, so by then we were already eating only organic stuff and the farm was in the process of going organic.'

'And there was nothing they could do for her?'

He shook his head. 'Only short-term and then it was all down to the Macmillan nurses and ultimately the hospice. It was agony to watch.'

Izzy could hardly imagine it. 'Did the children know?' she asked, thinking of the bright, bubbly young things who'd burst in on them just a few minutes earlier and chattered about coffins, of all things, and he nodded.

'Yes. Eventually. We told them she was sick, and then when it was inevitable and the end wasn't far away, we told them she was dying. She made them scrapbooks—snippets of herself for them to keep, memories they'd shared, things they'd want to know about themselves that only she could tell them. Some of it will only make sense to them when they're older, of course—things about their births, philosophical stuff about being a mother and what it meant to her—but lots of it was very ordinary and just things she'd treasured about them.'

Something splashed on Izzy's hand, and she blinked and swallowed. Tears. Tears for Julia, who'd always wanted to save the world, and for the children—and for Will, his voice quiet and thoughtful, telling her about Julia's last days. He had loved her, she realised with shock. Really, genuinely loved her. She hadn't wanted to believe it, but now she did.

She blinked again, squeezing the tears from her eyes and letting them fall, and then he made a soft, clucking noise with his tongue and handed her another fistful of kitchen roll.

She sniffed, scrubbing her nose with the tissue. 'I'm sorry. It's just all so sudden. I mean—I didn't even know until last night, and now, talking to you like this—it's all so real.'

'It seems light years ago,' he said gruffly. 'We move on. Time heals, Izzy. The kids don't stop growing just because their mother's died, and they've dragged me with them. I've had to cope because of them, and we've got through it together. It's been very positive in a lot of ways.'

'And all I've done is make rich people even richer and rescue reputations that probably didn't deserve rescuing, and acquire some of their wealth along the way. My God.'

Her voice sounded hollow, and it seemed appropriate. That was how she felt inside—hollow and empty and worthless.

'I shouldn't be here,' she said, the tears welling again, and then his arms were round her again— again!—and he was cradling her against his body, standing in front of her so her cheek was pressed against his board-flat abdomen, just above his belt, the buckle cold against her chin.

'Don't be silly,' he murmured gruffly. 'Of course you should be here. It's lovely to see you, Izzy. It's been too long.'

It had, she thought sadly. Much too long. So much too long that it was years too late.

Too late for what?

She didn't want to think about it—not with his belt buckle pressing into her chin and his arms around her and the solid beat of his heart sounding through that wall of muscle. And then his stomach rumbled, deafening her, and she laughed a little unevenly and eased away.

'You sound hungry.'

He laughed with her, propping himself on the edge of the table just in front of her and staring down into her eyes. 'I am. I missed breakfast—and, come to think of it, I don't know if I ate last night. I missed the food at the party. Come on, we'll go over to the café. Mum'll feed us.'

'In the café?'

'Mmm—the Old Crock. That's what she calls herself, and it seemed like a bit of fun to call the café the
same thing. She runs it—and the farm shop. Dad's in
charge of Valley Timber and the willow business.'

'The climbing frame and the tree house and the coffin,' she said, remembering Michael's words, and she
wondered uneasily where Julia was buried. The church-
yard, probably, since her father had been the vicar.
She'd have to ask him some time—but not now. Now
she'd heard and seen enough, and she needed time out
to absorb it all and put it into place in her head. And
her heart.

'He makes more than coffins. He broke his leg and
was in hospital, and he did basket weaving for occu-
pational therapy. He loved it, but it was a bit time-
consuming and not really cost-effective, and then he
discovered willow hurdles. It's all come from there,
really. But it's not just him; there are lots of people
working for him, many of them disabled. It's a thriving
business and it puts something back into the community, and we're all really proud of it. Come on. I'll
show you round after we've eaten.'

He held out a hand, large and strong and callused,
so different from the soft city hands she was used to,
and pulled her to her feet.

'It's changed so much,' she said as they went out
into the yard and she looked again at all the new enterprises.

'Not really. Not in the ways that matter. It's still
home.'

Home. Could he have found a word more calculated

to tear a hole in her heart? She thought of her apartment, high up in the polluted air above London's Docklands, with the deli and coffee shop and restaurant just inside the entrance, the health complex in the basement, the home shopping service, the weekly delivery of organic vegetables in a box to her kitchen, the concierge to run errands and fix stuff that went wrong— was that home?

A cow mooed, and under the bushes just in front of them chickens were scratching in the leaves.

No, she thought. *Not home. This is home.*

But not yours. Never yours.

'You're lucky,' she said to him, suddenly choked again. 'To live here, surrounded by all this.'

'I know,' he said softly, and she could see the pride and the affection in his face. Then he turned to her and grinned. 'Come on, come and see Mum. She'll be delighted to see you again. She loved you.'

You loved me. Or I thought you loved me. I loved you—

'I'll be delighted to see her again, as well. She's a darling,' Izzy said firmly, and, straightening up, she threw back her shoulders and headed across the yard beside Will.

CHAPTER THREE

As THEY crossed the farmyard, Izzy was struck by the hail of friendly greetings from everyone they passed. It was obvious that Will was well liked and respected by the community—and equally obvious that word of her presence here had spread like wildfire.

For the most part their friendly curiosity was harmless, and some of them remembered her family from all those years ago. They were kind and welcoming, if a little wary, which she could understand.

That dratted reputation again, she thought philosophically, and smiled back until her face felt like cracking.

Others, though, were not quite so tactful or kind— like the two old crones who stopped them just a few feet from the café entrance.

'What a lovely day, Will.'

'Isn't it?' he said, and made to walk on, but one of them stopped him with a hand on his arm.

'Aren't you going to introduce us to your friend?'

He sighed and gave a rather polite smile that made Izzy want to laugh.

'Sorry, ladies. Mrs Jones, Mrs Willis, this is Isabel Brooke.'

Mrs Willis nodded sagely, smiling at Izzy in a way that made her instincts prickle. 'Of course. You've been busy since you left here—the papers don't think much of you, do they, dear?'

44

Izzy smiled sweetly in reply. 'Don't they? I wouldn't know—I have better things to do than read the gutter press.'

The woman sucked in her breath, but any reply she might have made was drowned out by Will, coughing suddenly and turning away, and Izzy had to fight the urge to laugh.

'Sorry—choked—need a drink,' he gasped, and, grabbing her elbow, he steered her towards the café.

As they made their escape, Mrs Willis got her breath back. 'Well, really!' she muttered.

'Of course, they used to run around together—if you ask me, he had a narrow escape,' Mrs Jones chipped in. 'Julia was a lovely girl.'

Here we go, she thought. They're going to start on my mythical conquests in a minute.

A minute? They didn't wait that long.

'That one's a nasty piece of work,' Mrs Willis went on. 'Supposed to have a revolving door on her bedroom.'

'Oh, I believe it, and it isn't hard to work out what she's after now,' Mrs Jones said spitefully, her voice carrying clearly across the farmyard, and Will gave an exasperated sigh and shot Izzy an apologetic look.

'Hell, Izzy, I'm sorry,' he muttered. 'I didn't imagine even those two would be quite so harsh.'

She shrugged. 'Don't worry. I'm used to it. I've heard the revolving door joke so many times I'm immune,' she lied. And yet, even though she heard it every day, even though she was constantly sniped at by thwarted business rivals and the press took endless potshots at her reputation, still, to hear it up here in

what had always seemed like the ultimate sanctuary—
that hurt.

It wouldn't be so bad, she thought, if there was any
truth in it. If she had even one per cent of the fun she
was supposed to have, she wouldn't feel so hard done
by—and maybe that was the trouble.

'Come on, we'll get you a nice cup of coffee and a
menu to look at, and you can say hello to Mum. She'll
be pleased to see you.'

'Is she expecting me?'

'I told her I was bringing a friend in. I didn't tell
her who, but the rest of them seem to have found out.'

'Won't the children have said something anyway?'

'Maybe, but they probably got distracted and forgot.
We'll surprise her.'

Izzy was suddenly reluctant to enter the café. What if
Mrs Thompson felt the same way as those women—?

'Stop it. She loves you.'

'Does she? She must be the only one.' Izzy didn't
mean to sound so bitter, but after the latest barrage of
press coverage, weeks of working much too late every
night and trying to cram far too much into every day,
to have her morals raked over and be compared to a
dead woman and found so badly wanting was more
than she needed right now.

She was beginning to regret coming up here for the
party and was wondering how quickly she could make
her escape, but as Will ushered her through the door
of the café, Mrs Thompson looked across, put down
the coffee pot she was pouring from and came round

the counter, wrapping Izzy in a huge and very welcome hug.

'My darling girl, how lovely to see you!' she said warmly, and, holding her at arm's length, she studied her face, tutted and folded her back against her soft and motherly bosom. 'You've been overworking,' she chided, then released her, studying her again. 'But still as beautiful as ever.'

'You're very kind, but I know I look dreadful,' she corrected, unable to wipe the smile off her face. Her eyes were filling—again!—and that warm and motherly embrace was just about the last straw. She stepped back and looked around. 'Um—you look really busy. Do you want us to come back later?'

Mrs Thompson was having none of it, though. 'Good heavens, no, I'm never too busy for old friends. I'm taking a break,' she told her assistants. 'Coffee, Izzy?'

'Please, that would be lovely.'

'Three coffees, Jo, and we'll have it outside.'

Izzy didn't fancy that. It was warm enough, on this lovely April day, but she didn't really want to sit out there with those nasty old gossips in range and become the object of their continued attention.

Mrs T, however, had her own plan, and she ushered them out, settled them down in a sunny spot and fussed over Izzy so that it was clear to everyone that she was not only welcome, but *very* welcome.

And that, of course, was exactly what she was intending. 'Have those old bitches gone away yet?' she asked Will conversationally, and he gave a wry smile.

'I think so.'

'Good. I saw them homing in on you and knew they

were up to something. I think I might ban them. They're bad for trade.' She switched her clear blue gaze to Izzy and scanned her face thoughtfully. 'I'm sorry about them. I hope they didn't say anything too hurtful.'

Izzy shook her head. 'They've got a way to go before they can compete with the gutter press,' she said with a slight smile. 'I've heard it all before.'

'But not here, in your old home.'

For a moment she thought Mrs T meant the house, but then she realised she was talking about the village, and she felt a moment of confusion. Because if anyone asked her to define home, it would be the farmhouse she thought of…

'I don't really think of it as home any longer,' she confessed. 'My parents moved away during my first year at university, and—there was never anything to come back for.'

There was a sudden, awkward silence, then Mrs Thompson looked up at Will. 'Darling, go and chivvy up the coffee, could you? And ask how much of that pepper flan there is. I wanted them to save some for you; I know Izzy loves it.'

After a second's hesitation, he shrugged slightly and went, and Mrs T turned back to Izzy and took her hand. 'I'm really sorry about what happened that year. Julia was a wonderful mother, and she did everything she could to be a good wife to Will, but you were missed, Izzy—by all of us. Don't ever think you weren't.'

Oh, Lord. Her eyes were filling again, and she gave a shaky laugh and brushed away the tears with an impatient swipe. 'I swear I haven't cried so much since I was a baby,' she said with a vain attempt at lightness, but it blatantly failed and Mrs T clicked her tongue just like Will and patted her hand comfortingly.

'Poor girl. It's been tough for you, hasn't it? All the adverse publicity? Do they really think you're so hard and mercenary?'

Izzy shrugged and tried for another smile. 'I don't know. Does it matter? It's all good sport, I suppose.'

Again the tongue-clicking, and then she sat back with a smile as Will set the tray of coffee on the table, sat down again and sent Izzy a searching look.

'All right?'

'Of course I'm all right.'

'Of course she is—what did you think I was going to do to her?' Mrs T asked briskly, and handed Izzy a mug of steaming, fragrant coffee. 'Black or white, sweetheart?'

'Black, please. I think I could do with a shot of caffeine to give me back some spine!'

Will frowned fleetingly, but his mother was moving on with the conversation, leaning back in her chair and looking round. 'So, Izzy, what do you think of all the changes?'

She latched onto the impersonal shift gratefully. 'Amazing,' she confessed. 'I expected it to all be the same, but of course it isn't. Nothing's the same.' Rats. Back to that again.

She was conscious of two pairs of identical blue eyes homing sharply in on her, but she only spoke the truth.

What was it Will had said? Too much water under too many bridges?

And so much of that water in the form of tears—

She found her smile again. 'So—tell me all about the business. You run the farm shop as well as the café, Will tells me. When do you find time to sleep?'

Mrs T laughed. 'Oh, there are a few hours between midnight and dawn that come in handy.'

'She does too much,' Will growled affectionately.

'I always have done. I'm fine. I'm fit, I'm well and I'm active. That's all I ask. When I'm ready for my rocking chair, I promise you you'll be the first to know.'

Will chuckled and sat back, his coffee propped on his belt buckle, and Izzy dragged her eyes away from that firm, flat abdomen and the intoxicating fit of his jeans. She looked up and met his eyes, and something in their expression held her transfixed.

She'd seen it before, years ago, and it had been as mind-blowing then as it was now. Heat washed over her and she looked hastily away, pretending interest in the Valley Timber operation.

'So—how's your husband?' she asked Mrs T, and totally failed to hear the answer. All she could think about was Will, and the heat in his eyes, and the way he'd looked at her that long-ago summer...

He wanted her.

He'd always wanted her, right from the first moment he'd seen her when they were sixteen, but she'd been focused on her studies and had hardly noticed him.

Until that last summer. She'd noticed him then, and he'd engineered a camping party down by the river, and in a quiet moment, when the others were laughing and fooling around, they'd gone for a stroll alone together under the willows, and he'd kissed her.

Only once, then, and it had nearly blown his socks off. He'd retreated, shocked by the force of his feelings, and she'd blushed prettily and laughed and backed away, equally shocked. They'd got over the shock, though. Got over it and come back for more—and more, and more. Until one night, when they were alone in the house, he'd taken her to his bedroom and made love to her.

It had been a disaster that first time—he'd been fumbling, inept, and too eager to last more than a second or two, and she'd cried, not with pain but with frustration. So he'd tried again, and despite her shyness he'd learnt what pleased her, and it had blown his mind. Making love with Izzy had uncovered a tenderness and passion in him he'd never known existed, and he'd fallen head over heels in love with her.

From then on they'd been inseparable. They'd spent time with the others, but there had been no question that they were an item, and even though he'd planned six months of travelling round the Far East and Australia during his forthcoming gap year, he had seriously considered staying behind.

She'd considered going with him, but they'd talked it through, and in the end she'd stayed at home and he'd gone with Julia and Rob and Emma—and the rest was history.

He wondered how different his life would have been if he'd stayed behind that year, or if she'd gone too, if they would have been together, and he realised with something akin to shock that they wouldn't. Of course they wouldn't.

Look at them now—poles apart.

She lived in London, she was a mover and shaker in the business world, and he was a struggling farmer with two kids and a pile of paperwork so high he could scarcely see over it.

They had nothing in common, no meeting ground, nothing—except the lingering embers of a fire so hot it had burned in his heart for years.

And talking of hot—

He leapt to his feet, cursing softly under his breath and brushing at the searingly hot coffee he'd just slopped onto his jeans, a little below the belt and in a critical and highly delicate place.

Effective, though. It put the fire out even more efficiently than a cold shower, and after a moment of mopping and blotting he sat down again cautiously and shot them a wry smile. 'Sorry—I must have dozed off,' he lied, and avoided his mother's hard, knowing stare.

'Are you all right?' Izzy asked, concern in her eyes, and he just wanted to grab her and kiss her.

Damn. He all but ran his finger round under his collar. 'I'm fine,' he muttered, even though he wasn't. The coffee on his jeans was now cooling fast in the fresh April breeze, but even the combination of hot and cold wasn't enough to settle him down.

'I need to check on the kids,' he said, even though he knew they were perfectly safe, but he had to get away from Izzy for a moment and get his head in order.

'They're fine,' his mother said firmly. 'You sit down. I'll go and organise your lunch.'

And she walked off and left him alone with Izzy, not knowing where to look or what to say, conscious only of the heat rising up in him again and threatening to consume him.

Hell. It had been years since he'd even thought about sex—three long, tragic, lonely years—and now suddenly, like opening a door on a blast furnace, there it was, hot and raw and aching, and all because of this pretty and surprisingly vulnerable woman sitting beside him staring down unhappily into her coffee cup.

'I shouldn't be here,' she said, her voice soft, puzzled, and she looked up then, meeting his eyes, and a lump formed in his throat. Lord, she was lovely—and he was suddenly afraid for her. She seemed so vulnerable, so fragile, and now he could see the change in her.

That lovely, spontaneous warmth was tempered by caution, and he could see that the adverse publicity had wounded her deeply, making her uncertain and withdrawn. It was a tragedy, a crying shame, and he had to stop himself from reaching across and hugging her.

Or kissing her.

Instead he smiled, a crooked, slightly off-kilter smile that was all he could get past the emotion choking him.

'Of course you should be here. I'm sorry, I'm not being a very good host. Out of practice.' He put his coffee cup down before he did anything else stupid with it, and sat forwards, folding his arms on the edge of the table and leaning on them, to hide his misbehaving body. 'Tell me about what you do.'

'What I do? You know what I do. I'm an asset stripper.'

He snorted. 'Rubbish,' he said bluntly, and her eyes widened. 'I know you better than that,' he went on. 'You can't lie to me. Tell me about it. Why do you do it? And don't say for the money, because I know that's not true, either.'

She smiled reluctantly. 'For the challenge?' she offered. 'Because there's something incredibly satisfying about turning a company around and making it work when it's destined for the scrap heap?'

'So how do you know what to take on and what to leave?' he asked.

She shrugged. 'Instinct. A good product and lousy management and marketing are usually the keys. If the product's useless, there's no point, but if it ought to work and something's stopping it, then I'll take it on.'

'For a price?'

'Sure. And I'm ruthless. I try not to be unkind, but if someone's in the wrong job the chances are they aren't happy, anyway, so I don't have a problem with helping them relocate to something they're better suited to, either in the company or out of it. I have a recruitment agency as well, and I use that to help people find the right slot to fit them if I can.'

He chuckled. 'Be careful, you'll have me believe you're Joan of Arc in a minute.'

'Hardly. I can be pretty tough.' Her laughter was soft, and he felt a hard, tight knot in his chest ease a fraction at the sound.

'But not quite Godzilla.'

'Not quite.'

Their eyes met and locked, and he felt the heat again, searing through him, making him want things he had no business wanting, things he'd put out of his mind for years. Just when he thought he would have to kiss her or die, his mother appeared at his side, a tray in her hands and a beaming smile on her face.

'Here we are, darlings. Roasted pepper flan, green salad and fresh, crusty bread just out of the oven. More coffee?'

And that was it. They spent the next few minutes eating, and all he had to do was watch her tucking into her food as if she hadn't eaten for days. And for all he knew she might not have done. She was slim enough, goodness knows. If she ate like that all the time she'd be huge, surely?

And she certainly wasn't, although she went in and out in all the right places—

No! Not that again!

He pushed his empty plate away, wrapped his hand round his coffee cup and took a gulp of the fresh, scalding brew that brought the tears to his eyes and helped his mind to focus on something other than Izzy's body.

'Wow. That was even more gorgeous than I remember!' she said with a little laugh, and sat back, her plate scraped clean and her eyes alight.

She looked gorgeous, her mouth soft and full and moist with the sheen of oil from the salad dressing. How would it taste—?

'Fancy a guided tour?' he asked, smacking his cup down on the wooden table with a thud. The coffee slopped over the side onto his hand, and he winced. Perhaps he should give up on coffee for a day or two—

Her slender, eloquent brows pleated together over

puzzled, wary eyes. 'Am I holding you up? You must have things to do, and I'm taking hours of your time—'

'Don't be silly,' he said, feeling instantly guilty and hating himself for it. He tried for a smile. 'I'm sorry. I'm just used to eating and running—as I said, my social skills are getting rusty. There's no rush. Finish your coffee.'

'Your social skills are fine and I've had all I want,' she said, her mouth curving in a tentative answering smile that made the urge to kiss her even worse. 'If you're sure you've got time, I'd love a guided tour, but don't let me hold you up.'

'There's no rush,' he said again. 'Come on. My father will be looking forward to saying hello. He would have come over, but I expect he's busy keeping the kids out of mischief.'

'They seem full of it,' she said softly, and she sounded wistful.

Did she regret not having children? He didn't imagine so. Where on earth would she have fitted them into her lifestyle?

Where on earth would she have fitted *him* in, come to that, or vice versa?

Nowhere. They simply wouldn't ever have had time, either of them, and they didn't now. Not today, not any other day. This was strictly a one-off, and cherishing any illusions about seeing her again, about tasting that soft, ripe mouth or holding her firm, taut body in his arms was just a waste of breath.

He stood abruptly, scraping his chair on the paving and only just catching it before it toppled.

'Come on,' he said, more tersely than he'd meant to. 'Let's go and find my father.'

What on earth had she said? Something, that was for sure. His brows were dragged together in a frown, and he towered over her, big and intimidating and impatient.

She got slowly to her feet.

'I think I should go.'

'What?' His frown deepened, then cleared, and he sighed softly and gave a wry smile. 'I'm sorry. I'm assuming you've got time to burn and you're probably in a hurry to get back.'

'No. I just don't want to outstay my welcome.'

His eyes searched her face, and he sighed again and rammed his hands through his hair, tumbling the soft dark strands and leaving it spiked and unruly. 'You aren't. It's me. It's just seeing you again—bringing everything back.'

Julia, she thought. She was reminding him of Julia, of happy times when they were young, and she swallowed a sudden lump in her throat and straightened up.

'Come on,' he said gently, taking her elbow. 'You can't go without seeing my father, and I really would love to take you round the farm and show you everything we've done.'

He seemed to mean it, so with a little shrug she put away her doubts and smiled at him. 'I'd love that.'

'Then let's go.'

They crossed the yard to the old milking parlour, and his father came out with the children in tow. 'Isabel.

How nice to see you,' he said, and kissed her cheek lightly. 'You're looking well.'

'And you look just the same,' she said, scanning him quickly with affectionate eyes. A little greyer, perhaps a little more solid round the middle, but still the same man she remembered. He was a little shorter than Will—he'd been taller before, she thought, but Will had overtaken him, grown and filled out. They were still the spitting image of each other, though.

'I gather you've built an empire,' she teased gently, and he laughed.

'Someone's been talking it up,' he said wryly, and he led her through and showed her where they made the furniture and the garden toys.

'The toys are all modular—you can extend the climbing frames and ladders and make forts and tree houses and all sorts. And the timber's treated to last thirty years, so it's a pretty good investment.'

She looked at the play equipment, then at Mr T, obviously proud of his achievements, and nodded. 'It looks good. How do you market it?'

Two pairs of brows creased in a puzzled frown.

'Market it?' Mr T said. 'Well—people know we're here, they come and buy it.'

'So you don't advertise?'

'Locally, occasionally. We don't really need to do more.'

'And then there's the willow business,' Will said. 'So we've got more than enough to keep us occupied.'

She was sure they had. 'It's impressive,' she said honestly. 'Really good stuff. You should be proud of it.'

'We are,' Will said. 'Come and see the farm. Dad, are you OK to keep the children a little longer?'

His father nodded, and Will led her back to the house and round to the yard. 'We'll go in the Discovery,' he said, opening the door for her, and she climbed up into the big off-roader and strapped herself in, grateful for the space between them.

Or she would have been if it had been enough. Once he went round to his side of the car and slid into his seat, though, she realised that nothing short of a couple of miles would be enough.

Good grief! She hadn't realised the pull between them was so strong—at least, as far as she was concerned. She couldn't speak for him, and of course he was still grieving for Julia, so it was probably all one-sided.

She stifled the pang of sorrow and tried to concentrate on the maze of tracks he drove her down, pointing out all the things they'd changed, the crops they were growing, the difference because of going organic.

She tried to listen. She really, really tried to listen. But all she could hear was the sound of his voice, soft and low with a slight rasp of gravel now and then, and then they were heading downhill towards the river, winding their way around the fields until he stopped in the shade of the big old willows along the riverbank and got out.

She slid down from the car and followed him as he strolled slowly towards the water, pausing to pluck a blade of grass and twirl it absently in his fingers.

'We camped down here,' he said, his voice gruff. 'Do you remember? That summer?'

She nodded, unable to talk because his eyes were hot and tracking slowly over her, and everywhere they touched her, her body caught fire.

'I thought you'd be growing the willow here,' she said, struggling for normality but sounding breathy and desperate, like a sad old maid.

He shook his head. 'No. Not on this bit. I saved this bit.' He didn't smile. Instead he reached out, lifting a hand and brushing a callused thumb over her lips. 'I kissed you here, under this tree,' he said, his voice taut, and her breath jammed in her throat.

'I remember.'

They stood spellbound, trapped by something much stronger than themselves, and then he dragged himself free of the spell and strode back to the car.

'Will Thompson.'

His mobile. His mobile had been ringing, and he'd heard it.

She'd heard it too, but only dimly over the pounding of her heart. She realised she was holding her breath, and sucked in a great lungful of air, then another.

'We have to go,' he said tersely. 'I'm needed back at the farm—a ewe's in trouble.'

Not only the ewe, she thought with irony.

'Don't worry, I ought to be getting on anyway.'

He nodded, and before she was properly in her seat he was heading up the track, taking a shorter route back to the farm.

He slammed to a halt outside the house and turned to her, his hand on the doorhandle. 'I need to go and change and check this ewe,' he said. 'I'm sorry, I'd like to see you off properly, but I really—'

'Just go. Don't worry about me.'

He hesitated for a fraction of a second, then he leant over and pressed his mouth to hers in a hard, swift kiss that sent her pulse off the Richter scale.

'You take care,' he ordered gruffly.

'You, too. Thanks for today.'

'Any time.'

His door opened and slammed shut, and she was left sitting there watching him run towards the house. She followed slowly, retrieving her bag from the kitchen and scribbling him a note on the back of a business card.

Thank you for everything. If you're ever in London, here's my number. Be good to see you. Izzy.

And without further ado, without waiting for him to come down, she went back over to the café, thanked his mother for lunch and said goodbye, and headed back to London, her heart in turmoil. So much to absorb, so many things to take in and deal with.

Julia. The children.

And Will. Will, if anything even more attractive to her now than he had ever been, and even further out of reach. He didn't even have time for lunch and a little drive around the farm on a Saturday afternoon. What hope was there for any kind of relationship?

She lived in London, worked all over the country, sometimes out of it. On Monday she was flying out to Dublin to talk to a man about his ailing firm. She could be working there for weeks—months.

If Will didn't have time for a relationship, the same

was certainly true of her, because she was ridiculously busy.

And anyway, there was Julia, canonised in the village, her spectre hanging over the possibility of any relationship that they might have. How could she deal with that? Not even she needed a challenge that great.

No. She'd go back to London, and put Will out of her mind, and get on with the rest of her life.

CHAPTER FOUR

'SO—GOOD party?'

Will eyed Rob warily. 'You tell me—it was your party.'

Rob chuckled, his eyes altogether too searching for Will's peace of mind. 'Oh, I know what it was like from my point of view. I was actually talking about Izzy.'

Will knew perfectly well what Rob was talking about, and he had no intention of being led into such incredibly dangerous waters. Instead, he turned the tables on his old friend.

'Did you know she was coming?' he asked.

Rob shook his head. 'No—not when I last spoke to you. She got in touch a day or so later, just by chance.' Will's face must have showed his scepticism, because Rob threw up his hands in the air in a gesture of total innocence. 'Really, I swear. It wasn't planned—just a happy coincidence.'

Happy? Will wasn't sure about that. For the last couple of days he'd felt unhappy and unsettled, filled with a strange restlessness, and his nights had been rife with dreams. He didn't even want to think about those. Much too dangerous.

He made a noncommittal noise that didn't fool Rob at all, and made a production of looking at his watch. 'I have to get on,' he said, carefully avoiding Rob's

eyes, but the soft snort indicated that his friend didn't
believe a word of it.

'So, when are you seeing her again?'

Will stifled a sigh. 'I'm not.'

Rob stared at him. 'Why ever not?'

'What do you mean, why ever not? Why ever should
I?'

'Because there's still something there between you?'

Will rammed a hand through his already rumpled
hair, and glared at Rob. 'How on earth would you
know that?'

Rob shrugged slightly and smiled. 'Because I'm not
blind?' His smile faded, concern showing in his eyes,
and he scanned Will's face searchingly. 'I know you
loved Julia,' he said softly, 'but she's gone, Will, and
you and Izzy always had something special. I often
wondered—'

'Don't go there,' Will growled at him. 'It's none of
your damn business. Just keep out of it, Rob, I'm warning you.'

Rob threw up his hands in defeat and stood up, slinging the chair back underneath the edge of the table and
heading for the door. 'OK, OK, I know when I'm not
wanted, but just do me a favour. At least think about
it.'

He was out of the door before Will could reply,
which was just as well. He wouldn't have wanted to
hear what his old friend had to say about him. Then
Will sighed and pressed his lips together into a hard
line. Think about it? His laugh was short and bitter.
He'd thought about nothing else for days. He knew the
phone number by heart, he'd studied it for so long.

Several times his hand had reached out to pick up the phone, only to withdraw at the last minute.

Once, he'd even dialled the number and hung up before it could ring.

He was obsessed by her, tormented by the futility of his attraction for a woman so totally out of his reach. He wasn't fool enough to imagine it could be anything other than a passing physical attraction, at least on her side. If she felt anything at all, it was probably just curiosity, an urge to revisit once-familiar territory.

She was a powerful, sophisticated woman, and she would have better things to do with her time than spend it with a frustrated, overworked farmer—at least once that curiosity had been satisfied.

There was no way he was leaving himself open to that kind of heartache. Besides, he didn't even have time, so what on earth was he thinking about?

Izzy. That was what he was thinking about, all day and all night—she was driving him mad, and he almost wished he hadn't seen her again.

Almost.

With an impatient sigh, he pulled on his boots and coat, slapped his leg for the dog and headed out of the door. Forget Izzy, he told himself sternly. Forget the intoxicating scent that surrounded her. Forget the sound of her laugh, the soft curve of her lips, the gentle swell of her breasts.

But, try as he might, he couldn't forget the haunted look in her eyes when those two old bitches had been gossiping about her. She wasn't nearly as tough as she tried to make out, he realised, and for all her success

he'd sensed a strange restlessness in her, a lack of ful-
filment.

She seemed somehow sad inside, and he didn't think
it was simply because she'd just heard about Julia.
Instinctively, he knew it was more than that, and, fool
that he was, he wanted to reach out to her, to help her.
What on earth he thought he could do to help her he
had no idea, and anyway it was a crazy notion. She'd
probably find it highly amusing.

He climbed up into the tractor, the dog scrambling
up beside him, and fired up the engine. It started with
a roar that drowned out his thoughts, and just to be on
the safe side he turned on the radio good and loud and
listened to a political debate that was about as interesting as watching paint dry.

It was, however, a darned sight safer than thinking
about Izzy.

'Mr O'Keeffe, if I'm going to be able to help you,
you're going to have to provide me with a lot more
information.'

'Ah, Miss Brooke, but what information would that
be?' he asked in his soft Irish brogue.

Izzy stifled her exasperation and tried very hard not
to grind her teeth. 'Well, Mr O'Keeffe, until I have it
I won't know, will I?' She smiled sweetly at him and
thought if he answered with yet another question, she'd
probably have to stab him with the letter opener that
was lying on his desk.

Fortunately for both of them, he simply smiled enigmatically and pressed the button on his intercom.
'Deirdre, would you come in, please?'

His secretary came in with no evident haste, and eyed Izzy without curiosity. 'Yes, Mr O'Keeffe?'

'Miss Brooke would like some information,' he said. 'Do you suppose we could help her?'

'Now, then, which information would that be, Mr O'Keeffe?' Deirdre asked him innocently.

Izzy decided that if she didn't take the matter into her own hands, she was going to be there for the next five years just trying to get a glimpse into the filing cabinet.

'I'll need the last three years' accounts, financial reports, audit reports and sales figures—oh, and the personnel files.'

Deirdre's eyes widened. She looked worriedly at Mr O'Keeffe, but he merely raised his hands palm-up and shrugged.

'You heard the lady, Deirdre,' he said. 'She'd better have what she needs.'

And yet the information was not forthcoming. Deirdre couldn't find this, that was missing, the other was still with the accountant—the excuses were legion and relentless.

'Mr O'Keeffe, if I'm going to be able to help you, I'm going to need information,' she told him firmly. 'Now, either you are going to be able to provide me with that information, or I'm going to go home. I'm simply not going to be messed around by you any longer. Either you want my help or you don't.'

Deirdre was beginning to look faintly panic stricken, but Mr O'Keeffe seemed to take it all in his stride.

'Well, now, it seems we may have a little problem

there, Miss Brooke. Perhaps if you came back to-morrow—'

'I have a meeting in London tomorrow,' she pointed out. 'I have come here, as arranged, for a brief preliminary meeting to decide whether or not it's worth considering my involvement in the resuscitation of your company. Without information I can't do that, so it's up to you. If I leave you now, then I won't be back.'

He paused thoughtfully for a moment, then nodded to Deirdre. The woman left the room, and a few minutes later came back, her arms piled high with files.

Izzy eyed them sceptically. 'A CD or floppy disk would have done,' she said, trying hard to keep the sarcasm out of her voice.

'Ah, but there's nothing like a piece of paper for making things clearer,' Mr O'Keeffe said. 'Now, Miss Brooke, how about a nice cup of coffee?'

'I understand you want to talk to me, Mrs Jenks?'

'Well, actually it was me,' her son said, and Will could see from the way he squared up his shoulders that he was spoiling for a fight.

Not again, he thought with an inward sigh. Ever since they'd bought Mrs Jenks' farm and allowed her to live rent-free in her old home for the rest of her life, her son had been on Will's case. If it wasn't one thing, it was another. What was it this time? The windows? The heating system? The elderly Rayburn in the kitchen?

'About the Rayburn,' Simon Jenks began, and Will suppressed the urge to roll his eyes. 'Now the summer is coming, she really could do with it taking out and replacing with a decent cooker—'

'But I like the Rayburn,' Mrs Jenks protested. 'I don't want another cooker; I'm used to it.'

'But it's awful, Mother,' Simon said vehemently. 'It always goes out, you have to keep putting fuel in it all the time, and it's too much to expect of you in your state of health.'

She glared at her son. 'My state of health? What would you know about my state of health? You only turn up when you want to make a nuisance of yourself. I tell you, Simon, I like the cooker the way it is, and I don't want Will being put to a lot of trouble messing about and changing things just for the sake of it. I'm too old. I can't be bothered with it.'

Simon bristled a little, but was undeterred. 'Well—how about the windows?'

'How about the windows? The windows are fine. Simon, leave it,' Mrs Jenks said firmly. 'Now, if you've finished your coffee, why don't you go and get on? I'm sure you're very busy.'

He opened his mouth, shut it again and stood up abruptly. 'I'll pay for the coffee,' he said, but Will waved him away.

'Forget the coffee. It's on the house,' he said, and watched the man go with a quiet sigh of relief.

The sigh Mrs Jenks gave, on the other hand, was heartfelt and a great deal louder. 'Oh, that boy will be the death of me!' she said with a chuckle. She laid a gnarled old hand over Will's and patted it gently. 'You do know, don't you, that I'm quite happy with every-thing as it is? I'm an old woman, Will. I just want to be left in peace. I'm not interested in a new cooker or having the builders in. Don't let him browbeat you, will you?'

Will smiled at her understandingly. 'No, I won't let him browbeat me. I know he only wants the best for you, but sometimes when we're close to people, we can lose sight of what that is.'

The gnarled hands tightened on his. 'But you know, don't you?'

He turned his hand over and gripped hers gently. 'Don't worry, Mrs Jenks, I'll look after you.'

Her rheumy old eyes filled without warning, and she blinked and looked away. 'Oh, look, here are the children. I swear, they grow every time I see them. They were delightful earlier. I was talking to them when I arrived. Charming little things.'

Will looked at them, their eyes sparkling with mischief, and thought 'charming' wasn't perhaps quite the word he would have used. They were filthy, and the aroma drifting off them was something else.

He stood up and smiled down at the elderly woman. 'I think my charming little things need dealing with,' he told her dryly, 'if you'll excuse me?'

She chuckled, smiled benignly at the children and waved him away. 'Don't be too hard on them. They're just children.'

Just children? He nearly laughed out loud. Certainly they were children, but just? Just? Hardly.

He chivvied them across to the house, made them strip in the utility room and sent them to wash and change into clean clothes. They came down a few minutes later, smelling slightly better, and Rebecca said brightly, 'I like Mrs Jenks. She gave us some sweets. She said Simon is a pain in the neck. What's a pain in the neck?'

'She means he's a nuisance,' Michael said scornfully. 'I expect he wanted her windows mended.'

'No, actually, he wanted her Rayburn replaced,' Will told them, struggling to keep a straight face.

'I knew it was something like that,' Michael said. 'She was ever so cross with him.'

'He means well,' Will said, and closed the subject. 'So, are you two going to tell me how you got quite so filthy?' he asked mildly, and their faces were twin pictures of guilt.

'I dropped something in the pond,' Michael said, avoiding looking at his father. His tone was innocent enough, but Will wasn't fooled.

'Something?'

Michael shuffled unhappily. 'Beccy's shoe,' he confessed.

'And what were you doing with Beccy's shoe by the pond?'

'He stole it and ran off with it, and threw it at me, and it fell in the pond.'

'But I found it,' Michael said, as if that would make it all right again. 'It was a trainer, so you can wash it.'

'No,' Will said firmly. 'You can wash it.'

'Ah, Dad!' Michael wailed in protest, but Will was adamant. They had to learn the consequences of their actions, and if that meant scrubbing a stinking, filthy shoe retrieved from the bottom of the pond, then so be it.

He sent him off to do it, and Beccy, sitting at the

table scribbling with a pencil on the back of an old envelope, said innocently, 'Is Izzy your girlfriend?'

Will nearly choked. He opened his mouth to reply, then shut it again until he'd thought of something to say.

'Why on earth would you think that?' he asked after a moment, trying to keep a slightly wild note of panic out of his voice.

'Mrs Jenks said you were sweet on her. I didn't understand, so Michael explained.'

'Mrs Jenks said it was years ago, before you married Mummy,' Michael chipped in from the other room. 'She was talking to Grannie.'

How ridiculous to feel guilty for something that had happened so long ago, and yet, confronted by the innocence of his children, guilt was exactly what he did feel. Perhaps his recent thoughts and dreams were also partly responsible.

'She's an old schoolfriend,' he said firmly. 'I told you that.'

'But was she your girlfriend?' Beccy asked, reluctant to give up, but Will refused to be drawn any further.

'She's a friend—nothing more. Michael, have you finished that shoe yet? If so, you need to go over to the café and have some lunch quickly. You're going out this afternoon, don't forget.' And not a moment too soon, he thought, with questions like that cropping up right, left and centre.

'I wouldn't mind—I thought she was nice,' Beccy said, scooting out of the door before he could get another word in.

He gave a slightly strangled laugh. Nice? 'Nice'

wasn't the word he would have used. Gorgeous, maybe. Beautiful? Intoxicating?

Damn. Back to that again. He stomped into his study and flicked through his diary, checking the date of the next farmers' market, and a note caught his eye. There was a meeting in London, later in the week, about obtaining funding for certain organic projects, and he had pencilled it in without any real intention of going. He wasn't sure if it even applied to him, but it might be interesting.

And if he was going to be in London, then what would be the harm in meeting Izzy for a drink afterwards?

No. Too dangerous.

But as he went about his work for the rest of the day, the idea niggled at him, and by the time he'd put the children to bed at the end of the day, he could hardly think about anything else.

Just a quick drink—nothing formal or too elaborate. Keep it light.

If she was even there, of course, on Thursday evening. There was no guarantee that she would be. And anyway, he probably wouldn't even go.

It was just one of those days, Izzy decided. She'd waded through some of the paperwork she'd brought back from Ireland with her, and she still had far more questions than answers.

Not surprising, really, considering how evasive Mr O'Keeffe had been, but that still didn't help her to decide whether or not she was going to take up the challenge.

She was just debating phoning him and telling him where to stick his firm when Kate stuck her head round the door, her face alive with curiosity.

'There's a man here to see you. He hasn't got an appointment, but he's got the most gorgeous eyes. You ought to see him just for that!'

Izzy chuckled and leant back in her chair, swinging it round to face Kate and propping her feet on the corner of the desk. 'Gorgeous eyes, eh? Perhaps you'd like to give him coffee and keep him waiting so you can chat to him yourself?'

Kate laughed wryly. 'Love to, but it's you he wants. His name's Will Thompson.'

Her feet hit the ground so hard her ankles jarred. 'Will?' she squeaked, and hauled in a steadying breath. 'Will's here?'

Kate tipped her head on one side and eyed her even more curiously.

'Uh-huh. Still want me to entertain him?'

She stared at Kate. 'Um—no. Can you knock up some coffee?'

'You've got an appointment in twenty minutes.'

'With?' she asked, her mind completely blank.

'David Lennox. It's about the Dublin deal.'

The accountant. She paused for a second, then shrugged. 'I'll see Will—find out how long he's around. I may have to reschedule David.'

'He won't like it,' Kate warned, but Izzy shrugged again. David needed her business more than she needed him, and they both knew it.

'He'll live. Anyway, I'm not sure I'm ready to talk

to him—that paperwork's utterly impenetrable, and I think it's deliberate.'

She stood up, tugged her soft sweater straight and ran the tip of her tongue over her suddenly dry lips. 'Right. Let's see what Will wants.' She went past Kate, her heart hammering, and walked into the reception area on legs that had suddenly turned to jelly.

He was standing by the window, looking out over the city with a brooding expression on his face, and as she crossed the room, her footfalls muffled by the thick carpet, he saw her reflection and turned to her, one corner of his mouth kicking up in a wary smile.

'Izzy.'

'Will.' Her chest rose and fell rapidly. Crazy, but those eyes— 'What a lovely surprise.'

'I'm sorry, I should have called, but I was at a meeting today just a few minutes away from here, so I thought I'd drop in and say hi.'

She could feel herself smiling inanely. 'I'm glad you did. Come on into my office. Kate'll make us coffee.'

'Have you got time?'

'Sure,' she lied blithely. 'It's nearly the end of the day, and I haven't got anything important on.'

David Lennox wouldn't have thanked her for that, but it was just tough. And besides, the way Will's eyes were tracking over her put a whole new slant on her words. She was suddenly acutely conscious of what she *had on*—the soft cashmere sweater in the same muddy green as her eyes, the beautifully cut black trousers that did amazing things to her figure. And most particularly the fine silk and lace matching underwear she had put on this morning without any thought—

She swallowed and turned away from those searching eyes, leading the way into her office and closing the door behind them, then instantly regretting it, because now she was alone with him and—

'Izzy?'

She whirled round and stopped, trapped by those eyes, by the gentle puzzlement in them.

'I've just dropped in to say hi. That's all. I thought, if you weren't busy, maybe we could have a drink. But if you've got something on, don't be afraid to say so.'

Something on. Like the matching underwear? She closed her eyes briefly and feigned concentration.

'Nothing that I can think of. A drink would be lovely. Do you want coffee here first? How are you for time?'

He pulled a face. 'Time's fine. I can go on any train. I'll fit in with you, Izzy. I don't mind what we do.'

'We'll skip it, then—'

'Coffee,' her PA said, breezing in brightly at that moment and flashing Will a smile that made Izzy want to smack her. Good grief! The girl was besotted, and Will was smiling back, and she was—

Jealous. That was what she was. Jealous. How stupid.

'I've spoken to David—he was going to be late anyway, so you're seeing him tomorrow morning at seven-thirty. Will that be all right?'

Kate's question was seemingly innocuous, but Izzy read all the right meanings into it. Would she be available at seven-thirty tomorrow? Or still tied up with Will—?

'That'll be fine. Thank you, Kate. I think, though,

actually, we'll skip the coffee. I'm sure you can find some willing takers. I'm going to take the rest of the afternoon off. Can you field my calls and hold the fort?'

Kate grinned. 'I expect I'll manage. Have a nice time.'

Her dancing eyes showed exactly how she thought Izzy and Will were going to spend the afternoon, and Izzy was torn between whacking her over the head with the telephone directory and wailing with frustration.

She did neither. Instead, with considerable poise and sang froid, she unhooked her jacket from the back of her chair, slipped it on and smiled up at Will. 'Ready when you are. Where are you taking me?'

He laughed and rolled his eyes. 'It's your city. You tell me.'

She shrugged. 'OK. There's a little wine bar just round the corner that serves light snacks, unless you fancy anything a bit more substantial?'

'Sounds fine,' he said, and as they passed Kate, Izzy could see the curiosity bubbling behind those clear, intelligent grey eyes.

There'd be hell to pay for this, she thought, but suddenly she didn't care. She felt as if she were bunking off school, something she'd never done and had always fancied doing, and she had an overwhelming urge to throw back her head and laugh.

And then they were in the lift, going down to the foyer, and in the small confined space she was suddenly so utterly aware of him she could hardly breathe.

'Smart office,' he said into the silence, rescuing her just when she thought she'd start to hyperventilate.

'You like it?'

'Very impressive.'

She laughed. 'You have to look the part. Evidence of success is important, otherwise people think you aren't any good, but you have to get it right. Too much marble and gleaming steel and two-inch-thick carpet and they feel they're being ripped off—and God forbid they should realise the truth!'

He chuckled, the sound strangely soft and intimate in the enclosed space, and just when she thought she'd make a fool of herself the lift doors opened and they stepped out into the bustling foyer.

Will smiled at the receptionist. 'Found her,' he said, and Ally smiled back and coloured slightly. Another conquest, Izzy thought crossly, and resisted the urge to grab him by the arm and hustle him out.

Ally, though, didn't give her the option. 'So I see. Izzy, I've got something for you,' the girl said, and stood up and leant over, an envelope in her hand. 'This just came for you—Kate said you were on your way down.'

She took it, ripped open the envelope and scanned it, then stuffed it into her bag. It was another note from Steve. Really, she'd have to talk to him. Just not today.

'Thanks,' she said, flashing a smile at the girl. 'I'm not coming back tonight, Ally, if anyone calls, by the way,' she added, and Ally flicked an appraising glance at Will and smiled back.

'Sure. Have a great time.'

She didn't quite grind her teeth. Instead she made herself smile politely and whisked him out of the door.

CHAPTER FIVE

THE wine bar was heaving.

Izzy stared at it blankly, and Will thought she seemed flustered. Come to think of it, she'd seemed flustered since he'd arrived unannounced in her office, and now her composure was threatened again.

'It can't be this full. It's usually busy, but not like this. There must be an impromptu party or something.'

'It doesn't matter. We can go somewhere else, surely?' he said, trying not to sound too enthusiastic. Not that there was anything wrong with the wine bar, but a pub might be preferable. He might feel less out of place. As it was, amongst all the city types thronging the bar he was beginning to feel distinctly underdressed. His usual jacket and trousers had seemed fine this morning, and he'd put on his favourite tie. He'd even dug out a new shirt from the bottom of his drawer in honour of the occasion.

But, looking around him now, he felt like a country cousin, positively middle-aged compared to the frighteningly young executives swarming around them in pinstripe suits like upwardly mobile ants. There couldn't be anyone there a day over twenty-five, he thought in horror, and they were flashing credit cards around in their soft city hands, their designer watches and diamond-studded rings glinting in the sunshine.

Izzy stared at the crowd for another few seconds, then seemed to come to a decision.

'We can go to my place,' she suggested. 'There's a coffee shop and a restaurant in the complex, and I've got beer and wine in my apartment if you'd rather be there. I can probably find you something to nibble on if you're hungry.'

He didn't want to think about that one too hard.

'Your place sounds fine,' he said. 'I'd like to see it—so I can picture where you live.' That sounded dubious, so he qualified it hastily. 'I always think it's easier if you can visualise someone in their own environment. Sort of fixes them in their own place in the great scheme of things.'

And it would add another layer to his dreams.

Oh, hell.

'My place it is, then.' She shrugged, smiled and set off along the pavement at a fast clip, as if she wanted to hustle him out of sight of all the bright young things in the bar. She probably knew most of them, he realised—or maybe she was hustling him away from one in particular?

'Is there a fire?' he asked mildly, keeping up with her easily but just curious about her sudden haste.

She laughed and slowed down. 'Sorry. I always power-walk to work. It's good for me.'

He ran his eyes down her legs, clad in beautifully cut and incredibly sexy trousers, to her feet, and did a mild double-take. 'In those shoes?'

She looked down at the impossibly high heels and smiled. 'These? I always wear shoes like these to work. I need to look tall or people won't take me seriously.'

He snorted softly. 'I can't imagine that. They've only got to glance at your list of achievements to feel suitably intimidated. I'm sure your height's got nothing to do with it.'

'I just feel happier,' she said firmly.

'Whatever. I couldn't stand in shoes like that, let alone power-walk.'

Her grin was infectious. 'I'd love to see you try,' she teased, and he chuckled.

'I am not cross-dressing for your entertainment,' he retorted, and when she responded with a delicious gurgle of laughter, he suddenly began to relax. She was still Izzy, still capable of teasing him and having fun, and he stopped thinking about her meteoric success and concentrated instead on her and what she was saying.

'I nearly bought a place in here,' she told him, waving at a tall glass and brick structure that looked like an old industrial building.

He said so, and she nodded. 'It is. It's all very loft-style and open plan, but I didn't fancy rough blockwork walls and steel girders all over the place, and anyway, it didn't have a river view.'

And, of course, a woman of her substance would have a river view, he thought dryly.

You've got a river view, his alter ego prodded.

But in the country. That's different. And it's not quite the Thames.

They arrived at a discreet glass and steel entrance door in the side of a tall building. 'Here we are,' she said, and they went into the foyer.

His jaw must have sagged visibly, but he clamped his teeth shut and took it all in, in minute detail.

A broad, elegant sweep of marble served as a reception desk, concealing a uniformed security guard and a concierge, and off to one side a coffee shop, a restaurant and a little deli bustled with activity.

'We could eat here if you'd rather,' he suggested, hoping she'd disagree, and to his relief she shook her head.

'We're here, we might as well go up. Afternoon, George.'

The concierge smiled. 'Good afternoon, Miss Brooke. Your vegetable box arrived. I had it put in your kitchen.'

'Thank you. Any messages?'

'No. Just your post.'

He handed her a thick stack of envelopes, and she threw him a smile that would have ensured any man's undying devotion and led Will towards the bank of lifts on the opposite side of the foyer.

A man in gym gear with a towel round his neck appeared beside them and grinned at Izzy.

'Hiya, Iz. Haven't seen you in the gym this week. Everything all right?'

'Fine. I'm just busy. I will come, Freddie, I promise.'

'Mind you do. I don't want that shoulder playing up again.'

He winked at her and went off. Izzy stepped into the lift and swiped a card, and the doors hissed shut. Seconds later they opened, and Will followed her across a hall and through a door, opened with another swipe of the card.

Pale gold. That was what he saw. Gold from the sun on the walls, streaming through the floor-to-ceiling windows and flooding the room with light. And there below them was the river, stretched out in both directions and dotted with little boats.

'Come and see my garden and have a look at the view,' she said, and at the touch of a button the big doors slid open and she stepped out onto a roof terrace lush with plants.

He followed her and fingered a leaf thoughtfully, trying not to think how much such an apartment must cost to rent. He couldn't even begin to contemplate the freehold value. He glanced down at the slim, straplike leaf in his hand and recognised a cordyline. There was a yucca beside it, and beyond that a fatsia with huge, brilliant green leaves, startling against the concrete backdrop that was London. 'Nice plants. Watering them must be a nightmare,' he said, but she shook her head.

'There's an irrigation system. I'm away a lot. They'd die.'

Of course. What else? He crossed to the edge of the roof garden and leant over, peering down several floors to the riverside below. People moved like ants, and even the noise of the sirens and honking horns was muted this far up.

It was still there, though, and the air, although clearer, was still tainted with exhaust fumes.

He hated it.

He turned, brushing against a viburnum that responded with a wave of heady scent from the pink-blushed flowers, and he breathed deeply and the world righted itself. What a miracle, in this desert of brick and glass and seething bodies.

He touched it gently, almost thankfully, and went back inside, into the climate-controlled stillness of the apartment, and looked around.

Quiet understatement. Elegance, good taste and a great deal of money had created a beautiful environment. Only the teetering shoes cast aside on the rug and the bag dropped nearby on a butter-soft suede sofa made it look lived in, and he thought of his chaotic and untidy house and groaned inwardly.

What had she thought of it?

Of him?

Not that it mattered. If he hadn't realised before just how far apart their lives had taken them, he would have realised now.

'What can I get you to drink?'

He stiffened. Her voice was right behind him, so close he could hear her breathing. Or maybe he just imagined it. He stepped away, just to be sure, and turned.

'What are you having?'

She shrugged. 'Water, probably, for a start. I've got a water cooler.'

Of course. He looked across at the kitchen area of the big, open-plan living space and saw a gleaming steel American-style fridge with a water dispenser in the door, built into a wall of units in dark cherrywood.

'Sounds good.'

She laughed. 'You don't have to have water. You can have tea, or coffee, or beer, or wine—whatever.'

'Water's fine,' he said, and wondered how long they could continue talking about nothing when there was so much to say.

Or maybe there wasn't. Maybe it was all best left buried in the past, because the past was, after all, all they could ever have…

Will was looking distinctly uncomfortable. He'd downed the water as if he'd just been rescued from the desert, and she'd refilled his glass and gone over to the sofas, settling cross-legged into the corner of one and patting the cushion for him to join her.

'Mind if I sit here? I can see the river.' He shed his jacket and tie and took the other sofa, sitting with one leg hitched up, his ankle propped across the other knee, and, although apparently relaxed, she could feel the tension coming off him in waves. Because of her? Surely not. If so, why would he have come to see her?

He looked around, his face strangely expressionless. 'Nice place.'

Nice plants, nice place. She made a rude noise. 'You hate it.'

He blinked in surprise, but then laughed softly. 'No. I'd hate to live in it, which is just as well, since I wouldn't have a prayer of affording it, but I don't hate it. It's interesting—and if you're busy, and you've got to live round here, I guess this is the way to do it. I'm just glad I don't have to—not enough trees and animals for me.'

She could understand that. There weren't enough trees and animals for her, either, but that was one of the trade-offs. And if she needed trees and animals, she could go and find them easily enough. 'There's always the zoo,' she told him, but he winced.

'Not quite the same as having the cat on your lap while you're watching the telly in the evening.'

'No—but you don't have to feed them, either. I couldn't have a cat if I wanted one. I'm away far too much on business.'

He shook his head slowly from side to side, as if he was trying to understand. 'That must be hell. I'd hate to be away from the farm, but some of that is dreading the chaos I'll go back to.'

She laughed softly in sympathy. 'I can understand that. Luckily I have a brilliant PA—Kate. You met her. She keeps everything ticking over for me.'

He grunted. 'I need a Kate—think she'd come and work for me? I could pay her in eggs.'

Izzy chuckled at the thought. 'I think Kate might want rather more than eggs.' She tipped her head on one side. 'So what happened to all your plans? How come you ended up farming? You were so dead set against it. Surely you can't blame that on Julia and the baby?'

He gave a rueful smile. 'No. My father broke his leg just a few days before our wedding and ended up in a wheelchair for four months. I had to take over the farm, and by the time he was up and about again I'd realised it was what I wanted to do with my life.'

He settled back against the corner, some of the tension leaving his body, and she doodled in the condensation on the glass and watched him.

'So did you go to college?'

He nodded. 'Yes—the local agricultural college. It's attached to UEA in Norwich, and I did a degree in agriculture and land management.'

'Not quite the same as civil engineering.'

'No—but I'm happy, Izzy. I never thought I'd be happy staying in one place and doing one thing all my life, but now I can't imagine doing anything else.' He cocked his head on one side. 'What about you? Are you happy? All this—' He waved a hand around '—success. Has it made you happy?'

She looked down, suddenly struck by the realisation that, no, it didn't make her happy. It made her busy, and it made her rich, but happy?

Not in the ways that mattered.

'Mostly,' she replied, unwilling to give him total honesty. 'There are still things I want from life.'

You, for instance. To wake up to the sound of birdsong and find myself in your arms. To be pregnant with your child—

Good grief! That was too much honesty, even for her! She catapulted to her feet. 'I'm going to open a bottle of wine—what do you fancy? Red or white, or maybe something sparkling? We could break open a bottle of champagne, if you like. Sort of a late birthday celebration.'

He eyed her oddly. 'Red, please, if you've got any open. Nothing too heavy, though. I've got to drive when I get home.'

'I've got a nice light Merlot.'

He nodded. 'Do fine. Thanks. Want me to open it?'

He followed her to the kitchen without waiting for an answer, and she had the bittersweet joy of watching those strong, capable hands deftly stripping the seal and twisting out the cork.

He put the bottle down on the worktop just as she

turned with the glasses, and her elbow caught it. Only his lightning reflexes stopped it from crashing to the floor, and he righted it and smiled at her and her heart crashed against her ribs.

'Whoops.'

Whoops, indeed. He was standing just inches away from her, and as she watched, his smile faded. Very slowly, very deliberately, he released the bottle and moved his hand towards her face, turning it so that his rough, workworn knuckles grazed feather-light over her cheekbone.

'I've missed you, Izzy,' he said, his voice low.

She couldn't answer. Her heart was wedged up in her throat, and as he turned his hand again and trailed the tips of his fingers over her jaw and down to her suddenly dry mouth she thought she'd never be able to breathe again. Her tongue flicked out to moisten her lips, and she felt his thumb drag over the soft, damp skin.

A tiny moan escaped from her throat, and her eyes fluttered shut.

For what felt like for ever he did nothing, then his fingers slid round and threaded through her hair, anchoring her tenderly as his lips whispered over her jaw like the brush of an angel's wing.

'I've missed you,' he said again, his breath puffing softly against her cheek, and then his other hand wrapped warm against her shoulders and drew her to him.

She went willingly into his arms, her own stealing round him to cradle him against her heart as her lips parted for him and she felt again the gentle touch of his mouth settling on hers for the first time in so many years.

So sweet. So dear. So very, very welcome. She felt the coaxing invasion of his tongue, but there was no need to coax. She forgot all the reasons why this was a bad idea, all the reasons why she should run a mile.

She forgot Julia. She forgot the pain of losing him, the pain of knowing he loved another woman. She forgot the long, lonely, agonisingly bleak years without him.

And she forgot the sheer impossibility of a relationship with a busy man tied down by duty and responsibility and the demands of a farm and a family, not to mention her own duties and responsibilities and silly-hectic schedule.

Instead, she gave herself up to the warmth of his mouth, hard and yet yielding, demanding and yet giving so much more than he took. His body cradled hers, rocking her against him, and her body responded to his as a desert flower responds to rain.

And then he was releasing her, his hands cupping her face, his kisses light again, tender, soft little sips as he retreated, and she opened her eyes to find him looking down at her with regret and confusion in his eyes.

'I'm sorry. I don't know what I was doing.'

She tried for a smile. 'I thought you were kissing me,' she said, trying to make light of it, but all the reasons why it was such a lousy idea were crashing back into her scrambled brain like logs tumbling from a woodpile, and she pulled back, dropping her arms to her sides and resisting the urge to hug them around herself defensively.

He stared down at her sorrowfully. 'Izzy, I'm sorry. I shouldn't have done that.'

She turned away. The only way she could deal with the pain surging through her. 'Don't beat yourself up about it. It was only a kiss. It's hardly the first time.'

That wasn't the thing to say. She shouldn't have harked back to their earlier relationship. It was over, forgotten—or should have been. And yet wasn't that what this was all about? Laying the ghost?

Was that why Will had come here today? To lay the ghost? If so, his tactics were way off beam. Her ghosts, all of them, were running round her head screaming blue murder, and she gave her head a little shake to clear it.

'Wine?' she said brightly, and reached for the glasses.

'Thanks.'

He'd retreated, standing staring sombrely out over the river, his eyes hooded and his expression forbidding.

Idiot. Why had she thrown herself into it with so much enthusiasm? She could have kept it light, kissed him back and moved away.

No, she couldn't. Even she couldn't lie to herself like that. She'd been waiting for that kiss for twelve long years, and the moment he walked out of the door she was going to relive every precious second of it.

'Here.'

She handed him his wine and he took it, careful not to touch her, and retreated back to his corner of the other sofa as she curled into her usual place again and watched him warily over the rim of her glass.

'So—you never did tell me what brought you to London. You said something about a meeting?'

'Oh—yeah. It was a conference about ways of accessing funding for various farming initiatives.'

'Useful?'

He shrugged. 'Not overly. Quite interesting, but most of it was irrelevant to us.'

He fell silent again, giving the simple Merlot very much more attention that it actually warranted, and Izzy wondered what he was thinking.

Regretting the kiss, most probably, because until then they could have just picked up their friendship and carried on.

'I shouldn't have come,' he said suddenly. 'I thought I could do this—see you from time to time, chat with you, be a friend. But it's difficult. Much harder than I thought. We've got too much history to ignore it, and there's no way we could have a relationship now. We're just light years apart.'

He looked up from the wine and met her eyes, and she read regret and sadness in his gentle gaze.

'I don't want to have an affair with you, Izzy,' he said softly. 'It wouldn't be fair on any of us. So I think I'd better just go, and I don't think I should see you again for a while.'

'Another twelve years should do it,' she said, and even she could hear the ache in her voice.

His sigh was ragged and heartfelt. 'Izzy, I'm sorry.'

He got to his feet, set his wine down on the granite slab that served as a coffee table and came over to her.

'Don't get up. I'll let myself out.'

He picked up his jacket, tucked his tie more firmly into the pocket and then stooped and pressed a gentle, chaste kiss to her lips.

'You take care. And if you ever need anything, give me a call.'

'I thought we weren't going to see each other again,' she said, fighting to hold back the tears, but his hand touched her cheek and one spilled over and he brushed it away tenderly.

'I'd never turn you away if you needed me,' he said, his voice rough, and then he went, the door closing behind him with a soft click. She heard the faint whirr of the lift, and he was gone.

She brushed the tears away angrily.

'You're such a fool,' she told herself, scooping up the glasses and going into the kitchen to tip the wine down the sink. Freddie was right; she hadn't been in the gym for a while. She'd go and have a good work-out, and then a swim, and then she'd grab something simple to eat from the deli and have an early night.

'So how was the conference?'

'Oh—quite interesting,' he told his father, but couldn't for the life of him remember anything except seeing Izzy. 'I've brought some handouts back to look at.'

'See anyone you know?'

He nodded. 'One or two. I had a drink with an old friend afterwards.'

'Anyone we know?'

He felt his mother's eyes boring right through him, and he shrugged evasively.

'Don't think so,' he lied, and wondered if this was going to become a habit. 'Any phone messages? Anything happened I should know about?'

'Not really. The stock are all bedded down for the night. Why don't you stay for a drink?'

He shook his head. 'It's been a long day, and anyway, I need to get the kids home to bed.'

'Leave them here,' his mother suggested. 'They're in the middle of a video, and they're no trouble. It's the school holidays; it won't matter if they stay up late, and they love being here.'

'They love you spoiling them,' he corrected fondly, and gave in. He found them in the little television room, curled up under quilts, and kissed them both goodnight, then went back to the farmhouse and let himself in, Banjo at his heels.

'You're supposed to be an outside dog,' he told the animal, and was rewarded by a lashing tail and a swipe of a wet, pink tongue across his hand. He patted the dog's head absently and went upstairs and hung up his formal clothes, tugging on an old rugby shirt and a pair of worn jeans with a sigh of relief.

He could still smell London in his airways, hear the noise and bustle, feel the vibration of the underground trains coming up through his feet.

He didn't know how Izzy could stand it, although he had to admit she certainly made the best of it. Her apartment was hardly subsistence living, and she had the money to take advantage of all the shows and exhibitions and other wonderful cultural things that London had to offer.

If you could stand the press of people and the constant noise.

He pulled on his boots and went out with Banjo, doing the usual late check and then standing, arms folded on the top of the gate, just listening to the cacophony of sound that was night time in the countryside.

The owl swooped overhead again, as it often did, and his mouth twisted into a parody of a smile. He'd asked Izzy if she was happy, and she'd said mostly, or something like that. He'd told her he was, and yet he wasn't sure if it was happiness or contentment.

Recently, though, even contentment had eluded him, replaced by a strange restlessness.

Hormones? He'd been alone a long time, and before then Julia had been very ill for several months. No wonder he'd responded as he had to Izzy.

He shouldn't have kissed her, though. Big mistake. It had brought back all sorts of memories that were best left forgotten, and opened wounds that surely were healed by now.

And yet she'd cried. As he'd been leaving her, she'd cried, a solitary tear trailing down her cheek and nearly crippling him. He'd almost stayed, then. Nearly thrown away all his resolve and taken her back into his arms and made love to her.

He propped his hands on the top of the gate and hung his head, staring down at his feet and wondering if he would ever truly get her out of his system.

He had a terrible feeling that he wouldn't, and he wasn't even really sure he wanted to. At least this way he still had his dreams.

CHAPTER SIX

SHE went to Dublin on Monday, as promised, to see Daniel O'Keeffe.

Not that she held out any great hope of being able to work with him. The man was a nightmare, and she had a feeling she was simply acting as an expensive courier to return his impenetrable documents.

David Lennox had been suitably pithy about the lack of transparency in the information she'd been given.

'They're trying to pull the wool over someone's eyes. Maybe yours, maybe someone else's, but if I were you I'd steer clear. I don't like the look of them.'

The accountant never liked the look of any of the firms she took on, but she'd be a fool to ignore him on this one. Her instincts were screaming, and if she didn't get some straight answers today, she was walking.

Definitely.

'Forty-nine per cent?'

She sat back in her chair, folded her arms and met his eyes fair and square. 'Forty-nine per cent. I'll give you my time for nothing, and at the end of the day, if my strategy's failed and the firm's in the state it's in now, I'll be out of pocket. If it works, and I believe it could, we'll all be a lot richer.'

'Fifteen.'

She laughed. 'Not a chance. I wouldn't do it for

fifteen per cent if it was a dead cert, and the only certain thing about your operation, Mr O'Keeffe, is that
nobody will give me a straight answer to my questions.
I don't like that—it makes me uneasy.'

Her words made him uneasy, too, for all the charm
and the ready smile. She was getting too close to something, and all of a sudden the hairs on the back of her
neck started to prickle.

'Tell me about Cork,' she said, and if she hadn't
been watching him so carefully she would have missed
the tiny flicker of alarm in his eyes.

'Cork? Ah, now. Beautiful place. Beautiful county—
wonderful scenery. You'd love it—'

'I wasn't asking for a tourist information sales pitch,'
she told him dryly. 'I was curious about your transac-
tions with a firm there—DOK Logistics. You see, I
can't find any record of them. I just wondered if you'd
care to shed any light?' Yep, he was definitely looking
shiftier by the minute.

'You can't find the records? How strange. They're
there, to be sure. You must have looked in the wrong
place. Haulage firm. We use them from time to time.'

'Expensive haulage.'

'You have to pay for the best,' he assured her, but
he couldn't quite meet her eye, and she hadn't got past
the fact that DOK just happened to be his initials.

'I don't need this,' she told him, finally coming to
her senses. She didn't need the money, it was too big
a risk, and she didn't trust him. He had all the charm
the Irish were renowned for, but he was lying like a
rug and she'd had enough.

She stood up, clipped her briefcase shut with a de-

fiant click and held out her hand. 'Goodbye, Mr
O'Keeffe. I hope you find someone to help you sort
yourself out—I'm afraid it won't be me.'

He looked at her hand for a long moment, then gave
a wry smile and stood up, shaking it gravely. 'I'm sorry
we won't be doing business. I was looking forward to
it. Thank you for your time.'

Looking forward to the money, more like. And as
for her time—! 'My pleasure. I'll be sending you my
bill.'

Not that she had any hope of it being paid, but it
was the principle—something O'Keeffe seemed a little
short on, for all his charm.

She took a taxi to the airport, took the first available
flight and landed at Stansted airport at four that afternoon. The sun was shining, but the ground was soaking
wet, and as they were transferred to the main terminal
building from the arrivals satellite they were informed
that there would be hold-ups in getting away from the
airport because torrential rain had caused havoc and the
county's roads were gridlocked due to a spate of major
accidents.

Great, she thought. Just when she was looking forward to getting home and having a nice cup of tea and
a long, hot soak in the bath.

She had no luggage to collect, so she headed straight
for the exit to find out just how bad the situation was.
One look, however, at the mass of people thronging
the information desk and stacked up outside all the
food outlets, and she had her answer.

There was an information board giving further details, and as she walked she stared up at it, silently

cursing herself for ever getting involved with O'Keeffe.
If she'd followed her instincts—

She didn't see the ice cream the child had dropped.
She found it, though. One minute she was striding towards the information board, the next she was on the
floor, her arm doubled under her and pain like she'd
never felt in her life surging through it, robbing her of
everything except the need to die.

Will walked into the kitchen, glanced at the answer-
machine and saw the blinking light. He sighed.
Probably something else he'd forgotten to do, he
thought with resignation, and hit the 'play' button.

'Will? This is Izzy. I was just ringing to hear a
friendly voice. I'm stuck at Stansted—I've fallen down
and broken my arm, and I can't get an ambulance for
hours because the roads are in chaos and all the hos-
pitals are implementing their major incident plans because of the rain, and I hurt, and I just wanted to talk
to you. Sorry, I'm rambling. I'll go.'

Her voice had a quiver in it he didn't like, and it
rose towards the end, as if she had been struggling for
control. He frowned at the answer-machine, pressed the
button to listen again, then dialled 1471 and called her
back on her mobile.

She answered after a few rings, sounding woozy, and
his concern accelerated. 'Izzy? What's going on?'

'Oh. Hi, Will. Sorry about the pathetic message. I
was just feeling a bit lost. I couldn't get Kate, my PA,
and I just wanted to hear a friendly voice, really.'

Her voice wobbled, and he felt the adrenaline begin
to pump round his body. 'Tell me about your arm,' he

said, wanting her to focus and needing to know how bad she really was. She sounded horrendous. 'Izzy? Talk to me.'

There was a pause. 'Well, it's—broken.'

'You're sure?'

Her laugh was slightly manic and worried him. 'Oh, yes,' she said. 'It's sort of bent, just above my wrist, and it hurts.' Her voice wobbled again, and she went silent.

'How's the traffic situation? Any news on your ambulance?'

The laugh was definitely desperate this time. 'Oh, it gets worse. About seven hours, they think. I don't think I can sit here for seven hours—well, that's silly. Of course I can. I don't have a choice. I wonder if there are any heroin addicts about that want to share?'

His imagination ran riot until he realised she was joking. 'Haven't they given you anything for the pain?' he asked, wincing as he imagined what she was going through.

'Oh, yeah. There's a paramedic here, and he's been brilliant. He's had a look at me and said it needs hospital, but I just can't get there, so I'll have to wait. All the roads are at a standstill; it's hopeless. I've had some pain relief, but nothing short of oblivion will be good enough for a while, but it's better than it was and at least it's in a splint. I'll live.'

'Where are you?' he asked, an idea forming in his head.

He could almost see her shrug. 'Oh, I don't know. In some office somewhere in the main terminal. At least it's quiet. It's bedlam out there. Will, don't worry.

I'll be OK. Look, I have to go; my battery's getting low and I might need it. I'll speak to you later.'

She cut him off, and he stared at the phone for a second, then punched in another number. Two minutes later he'd made the arrangements, changed into clean clothes and headed out of the door.

'Izzy?'

She opened heavy lidded eyes and stared blankly at him. Was he real, or had she conjured him up out of the drug-induced haze that was enveloping her? Whatever, he was the most welcome thing she'd seen in a long while, and she reached out her good hand, the one that wasn't dying with pain, and touched his hand. It gripped hers back. Real. Amazing.

'Will?'

'That's me.'

She tried to think, but it was too hard. There was something, though. Something important. Yes, that was it. The roads. 'How did you get here?'

His grin widened and he crouched down in front of her and pressed her fingers to his firm, warm lips. 'Friends in high places,' he said enigmatically. 'Come on, I'm taking you home.'

She thought she'd never heard anything so wonderful in all her life, but she still had no idea how he could do it.

'How?' she asked, puzzled and unable to think clearly because of the painkillers.

'Same way I got here—helicopter. Told them it was a mercy mission—got air ambulance clearance to land.'

'You've got an air ambulance?' she said incredulously, but he just laughed and shook his head.

'Not quite. It's Rob's brother's toy. Remember Andrew? I twisted his arm.'

She winced at the thought, and he pulled a face. 'Sorry. Inappropriate metaphor. Luggage?'

She shook her head. 'No luggage. Only that bag.'

'Come on then. Your chariot awaits, ma'am.'

She stood up and swayed, and he took her good arm firmly and clamped her against his solid and very welcome side.

'Whoops,' she said, and tried to smile, but the room was spinning. She sat down again abruptly, and after a moment tried again.

'OK now?'

She nodded. 'Better.'

'Come on, then, Dizzy Izzy,' he said with a tenderness that brought tears to her eyes. 'Let's get you out of here.'

There was a car waiting for them, and they were whisked across to the north side, to the old terminal building the private flights operated from, and within moments she was strapped into a seat in a little helicopter and Rob's brother Andrew was grinning at her.

'I've always wanted to rescue a damsel in distress,' he said with a laugh, and she smiled back weakly and sagged against the seat.

'Happy to oblige,' she said, but her voice sounded slurred with pain and drugs, and saying anything else was just too much effort.

Will strapped himself in beside her, and held her good hand while Andrew went through the pre-flight checks, then got clearance for takeoff. There was that horrible sickly moment when the aircraft tipped forward and surged away from the ground, and then everything righted itself again and she could see straight.

Well, straightish. The painkillers must be something else, she thought, and closed her eyes. The vibration of the helicopter was giving her arm grief, but in what seemed like seconds, but was probably minutes, they were setting down in what looked like a playing field.

'Where are we?' she asked, puzzled.

'Ipswich Hospital—well, a school right behind it. Look, there's someone there with a stretcher.'

She sighed quietly with relief. She didn't want to make a fuss, but her legs didn't really seem to belong to her, and the idea of lying down was starting to appeal more and more.

Will helped her down the steps out of the helicopter, the person with the trolley manoeuvred it under her, and as she sat down on the edge of it everything faded away and went black.

'Will?'

Her eyelids fluttered open, and he leant forwards and took her good hand, glad to see her back in the land of the living. 'Hi, there, Sleeping Beauty. How are you feeling?'

'OK. You must be tired, all this hanging around. What about the children?'

'With my parents. Don't worry about them. How are you, really?'

'Sore. Hand hurts.'

'That's because they've sedated you and straight-

ened your arm. You've got a temporary cast on, but
you've got to go down to Theatre tomorrow and have
an operation to pin it.'

She blinked and stared at him, trying to focus.
'Can't. I've got a meeting—'

He laughed and shook his head. 'Not any more, you
haven't. Sorry, old thing, you're out of commission for
a few days at least. They'll let you out tomorrow evening, if you're all right and have someone to look after
you.'

'But—where will I go?'

'Home with me,' he said firmly. She opened her
mouth to argue, shut it again and smiled weakly.

'Thanks.'

He nodded. 'My pleasure. Now, you need some
sleep, and so do I, but I'll see you in the morning.'

He pressed a chaste and friendly kiss to her forehead,
and went quietly out, leaving her alone.

Silly. She missed his presence even while she could
still hear his footsteps retreating down the hallway...

She didn't want to go through those next few hours
and days ever again, Izzy thought when she woke on
Wednesday morning. She could hardly recall the pre-
vious thirty-six hours, but there was a lingering memory of pain and hideous nausea, and through it all Will,
beside her whenever she woke, holding her hand, holding her hair when she was sick, holding a glass and
making her drink cool water—holding her together.

She opened her eyes, and for the first time in what
felt like days she was alone. How silly, to feel that
sudden emptiness because he wasn't there.

He had work to do, a farm to run, children to take to school—or was it the holidays? She didn't know for sure. Not being a parent, she was out of touch with these things. They'd need feeding and dressing, though. Did you dress children of ten and eight or whatever they were? She had no idea.

She looked around the room, taking in the simple furnishings and restful colour scheme. Pale blues and creams, with old honey pine furniture that looked hand-waxed. By Will? Maybe. She was in a double bed, the mattress gently supportive, the quilt softly snuggled round her. Was that why she'd slept so well, or was it the painkillers? Probably.

There was a pretty chair in the corner, and a robe was laid over the end of the bed. Not hers, because all of her things were in London, but someone's.

Julia's?

A chill ran over her. Had this been their room? Or had Julia decorated it, not knowing that Izzy would end up here, staying in it?

She threw back the quilt and sat up slowly, swinging her legs over the side of the bed and pausing while the world righted itself. She really didn't need to fall over again.

'Izzy?' There was a tap on the door, and Mrs T poked her head round and smiled. 'You are awake. I thought I heard you move. I was in the kitchen down below you. How are you feeling?'

She gave a wry smile. 'I don't know. I'll tell you when I try to walk. I need the loo.'

'And a cup of tea, I expect, in that order. Here, slip this on. It's my spare dressing gown—the respectable one I keep in case I have to go into hospital. It'll probably drown you, but it's not full length so you shouldn't trip up in it.'

Izzy slid her good arm into it, relieved that it wasn't Julia's, as she'd feared, and Mrs T settled it around her shoulders over the baggy old T-shirt that was probably Will's, and helped her to the bathroom just next door.

'I'll be in your room, straightening your bed. Give me a call if you need me,' she said to Izzy. 'Oh, and there's a toothbrush and toothpaste on the windowsill for you if you want them.'

'Thanks,' she said, touched by their thoughtfulness.

She managed without help—just. It was the silly things, though. How did you tear off the loo paper with one hand? Fortunately the fracture was in her left arm, because she was most profoundly not ambidextrous, but even so it was a nightmare.

Pulling up the hospital-issue paper knickers. Squeezing the toothpaste. Drying one hand without the other to help.

Weird. Very unnatural. It dawned on her that her plan of going back to London either today or tomorrow might be a little ambitious.

Which posed a problem, of course, and one she'd have to discuss with Will when he reappeared.

She went back to her room, to find that Mrs T had fluffed up her pillows and propped them up, and turned back the quilt so she could get back into bed easily.

She eyed the bed with longing, but she was hungry and thirsty and she ought to get dressed and think about breakfast.

'Come on, back into bed and I'll bring you up something nice. What do you fancy?'

She felt her brows pleat a little with worry. 'You haven't got time to run around after me.'

'Nonsense. I've got lots of staff over at the café. Let them earn their keep. Now, what'll it be? Tea, coffee, or something milder? We've got green tea, or fruit tea of various denominations, or I can find you some fruit juice?'

'Tea, please, if you really have got time. Just ordinary tea, not too strong, not too milky, no sugar. That would be lovely.'

'And what about something to eat?'

She opened her mouth to say she wasn't hungry and her tummy rumbled.

'I think that's a yes,' Mrs T said with a chuckle. 'Come on, back into bed and I'll see what I can find. Will's cupboards tend to be a bit bare, so I might have to nip over to the café. I won't be long.'

Will's cupboards? She went out, leaving Izzy to think about that one. She'd assumed that all of them lived together, but maybe they didn't. How odd, to think of Mr and Mrs T anywhere else. And that meant she was here alone with Will and the children.

A little shiver of something ran over her, and she bit her lip. Not that he was about to take advantage of the situation with her arm in plaster, but it made her feel uneasy. What would those old busybodies in the village be thinking of her? Of them?

She rested her head back against the pillows and stared blindly out of the window. All she could see was rolling fields stretching away into the distance, punctuated by woodland and hedges that criss-crossed the landscape like seams on a patchwork.

Beautiful. The window was open, and she could hear the lambs bleating outside. She sat up and peered down, but the angle was wrong. Was Will out there with them? Maybe.

She leant back again, conscious of the pain in her arm and a slight prickling where the wires holding the bones together came out of the skin. At least, she thought that was what it was, but her memory of the post-op chat with the doctor was patchy and she didn't really want to think too much about it. She concentrated instead on keeping her hand very still.

Mrs T reappeared in the doorway, a tray in her hands, and settled it on the bedside table. 'Tea, and fingers of French toast with honey. You always used to like that.'

How amazing that she remembered. Izzy smiled her thanks and wriggled further up the bed, taking the tea she was offered and sipping it gratefully.

Odd how nothing in her life had ever tasted so welcome. Before she knew it the mug was empty, and she rested it down on her lap and smiled at Mrs T. 'Gorgeous. I was ready for that.'

Mrs T's smile was approving. 'Good. Now, tuck into this and see if we can't get a bit of colour back into your cheeks.'

She handed Izzy the pile of French toast, cut into convenient fingers so she could manage it with one hand, and while Izzy ate she told her that Will was out on the farm with the children, checking the fencing over at the Jenks side of the farm, because he was going to move the sheep over there now they'd finished lambing and were all outside again.

'The name's familiar. Do I remember Mrs Jenks?' she asked, and Mrs T shrugged.

'Probably. She's always been around. All my life, certainly, and probably my mother's, too. She's a wonderful character, and what she did to deserve her son I can't imagine. He's such an old woman. She sold the farm to Will on condition she can live there for the rest of her life, and her son nags him constantly to replace the Rayburn in the kitchen and change the windows and refit the bathroom, and she doesn't want to know.'

'So what does Will do?'

She laughed. 'Nothing. And then the son thinks he's being a negligent landlord—even though he chases round after her and is there more often than her own son. And not only does he not charge her rent, he provides her with wood cut to the right size for her stove and stacks it just by the door. He clears her snow in winter, cleans her windows, takes her shopping—he's wonderful to her, and her son just drops in from time to time and complains.'

'Why doesn't Will tell him to take a hike?' Izzy asked in astonishment.

Mrs T just looked at her. 'Because he's not like that. He says the son's just concerned, but he's not. He's trying to milk the deal for all he can, even though he's got his hands on the money for the farm already, from what I've heard. I try not to listen to the gossip, but there's a lot of it, of course, in the café.'

Which reminded Izzy of the two old women who had been so bitchy the last time she was here.

'Mrs T, is my being here going to be a problem for Will? I mean, with the village? People will talk, and I don't want to cause trouble.'

'Good grief, child, you've broken your arm! Of course you're here; you need help. You can't possibly manage on your own.'

Nobody had called her a child for years, and Izzy had to struggle not to smile. There was something comforting about it, though—about being taken care of generally. Nevertheless, she was still worried about Will's reputation, and she needed to know about his domestic arrangements.

'You said something about Will's cupboards. Do you not still live here?'

Mrs T shook her head. 'No. When he and Julia got married they took over one of the estate cottages, and when they had Rebecca, and the people in the other half left at around the same time, it seemed sensible to knock the two halves together and make one decent-sized house. When Julia got very ill, they moved in here, and she had a room downstairs until she had to go into the hospice.

'Then last year, when the children seemed to be coping without her, and because Will needed to be here running the farm and we didn't, it seemed to make sense for us to take over the cottage and leave the house to him. Peter said us being here might cramp his style, and they needed to be independent, but we aren't far away and we muddle along somehow.'

She patted Izzy's hand. 'Don't worry about the gossips. You leave them to me. Our house is too far from the café for me to pop across like this and keep an eye on you if you were there, and Will's busy so he can't do it. Anyway, it won't be for long, and it's lovely to have you here, so don't you give those silly old gossips another thought. You just concentrate on getting better. More tea?'

And that was the end of that.

She ate her breakfast, drank two more cups of tea and then Mrs T left her to sleep.

She did, as well, to her amazement, but not for long. Her young, fit body was recovering fast from the shock and the anaesthetic, and, rather than sit there and think about how much her arm hurt, she got up and went over to the window and sat on the wide sill and looked down at the sheep.

She was still sitting there when Will came back with the children, and he looked up at her window and waved at her, and she felt as if the sun had come out.

How foolish. Less than a week ago he'd been at pains to point out to her that there could be no future for them, even in the short term, and now here she was, a guest in his house, utterly helpless and unable even to dress herself without assistance!

So how was that going to work?

She had no idea. All she knew was that she wanted to be here—no, needed to be here. Her body needed to rest and recover, and so did her heart. It had been years since she'd done nothing for a while. Two years since she'd taken so much as a few days off.

It wouldn't hurt her now.

But Will might. He'd hurt her before, and she wasn't foolish enough to believe he couldn't do it again.

Would she survive this time?

She got up and walked back to the bed, her legs a little unsteady, and moments later she heard him run up the stairs two at a time. There was a knock on the door, and it opened a crack.

'Izzy? You decent?'

She chuckled. 'Not according to Mesdames Jones and Willis, but I'm covered from neck to ankle. You can come in.'

The door swung wider and he appeared, his smile apparently warm and genuine. 'How are you?'

'Fine,' she lied. She could have said she'd missed him when she'd woken, but there was no way she'd confess to being so pathetic and needy, and anyway, if he didn't want a relationship, she had no intention of pushing it.

'Did Mum look after you?'

'Of course. Don't you trust her?'

His smile grew wry. 'Sorry. Of course she did. I expect she forcefed you.'

'Almost,' Izzy admitted with a grin. 'Tea and French toast. She remembered I love it.'

'She's like that.'

He perched carefully on the end of the bed and pursed his lips, studying her. 'You OK, really?'

She shrugged. 'Hurts a bit. I'll manage.'

'That was never in doubt. You ought to let go, you know—let someone else take over for a while.'

Her smile was slow. 'I'm a control freak. It's hard for me.'

'I know, but sometimes things happen that are bigger than us, and we have to go with the flow.'

'Like breaking my arm and ending up here? I really

only rang you because I just felt so stranded and lonely. I didn't mean to trouble you, especially after what you said about not seeing me again for a while. I'm sure you didn't mean four days.'

He made a sound that was half-laugh, half-sigh, and rammed a hand through his hair. He looked away, then looked back, his hand locked around the back of his neck, and the teasing light had gone from his eyes. 'I said if you ever needed me, give me a call. I meant that, Izzy. I really meant that, and I'm glad you felt you could do it.'

'You also meant what you said about not seeing me again, though—didn't you?'

He shrugged dismissively. 'Forget that. You needed getting out of there fast. It was a hellish situation, and I only did what any friend would have done.'

'And if I'd thought about it I could have arranged a charter flight myself into City Airport, got a taxi to a hospital in London, then gone home the next day.'

'And then what? How would you have looked after yourself? You aren't dressed yet. Can you do it?'

She thought of her clothes—the jacket they'd had to cut off her in Casualty, the trousers with the side zip that she'd never reach with her other hand, the blouse with the fiddly buttons. Not a chance. She didn't even know where they were.

'I'd have my tracksuit bottoms and a baggy T-shirt at home,' she reasoned, and he got off the bed and went out, coming back a few minutes later.

'Michael's jog bottoms and a rugby shirt of mine that's shrunk in the wash. Fresh socks. I think Mum washed out your underwear. If you can manage to get that lot on without help, you'll be doing well. And how would you cook, and shop?'

She shrugged again. She seemed to be doing that a lot lately. 'I wouldn't. I'd eat downstairs, or get stuff sent in.'

That was the easy bit. It was the other things she was beginning to wonder about, like doing up her bra and opening jars and cans and all the things one just took for granted. Washing. Showering. Hair-washing. That was going to be interesting, with her hair turning into a scouring pad at the first sign of water.

'Not easy, eh?'

Was he reading her mind? Probably. He used to.

'I'd manage,' she said again, more firmly. 'And, talking of rescuing me, that kind gesture—for which, by the way, I'm profoundly grateful, because I don't know how much longer I could have stood it—must have cost someone a small fortune in fuel and airport fees. You must let me know how much, and who I owe, so I can sort it out.'

'Andrew,' he said. 'But don't worry. He owes me shedloads of goodwill. He keeps his helicopter here on the farm. We'll call it rent.'

'Then you should have it—'

'Izzy,' he growled warningly. 'Let it go. It's not often I get to play the hero. Just let me do it, eh? Just this once?'

She felt the smile start at her toes and work its way up.

'My pleasure,' she said. 'Now, if you'll find me my underwear, I'd like to get dressed.'

And, of course, she'd forgotten it was the little

scraps of Janet Reger. He came back in with the tiny garments dangling from a fingertip and a smile lurking in his eyes.

'Underwear?' he said questioningly, and she pressed her lips together to keep in the sassy retort and snatched them out of his hand.

'Thank you. You can go now. I can manage.'

His lips twitched, but without a word he turned and went out.

'I'll be here when you need help,' he said, and it was all the challenge she needed.

The bra didn't make it on—much too hard—but the little lace thong and the rest of the clothes she managed, with some difficulty, and when she emerged on the landing, sore and exhausted but victorious, his smile was one of reluctant admiration.

'Stubborn woman,' he said gently, and brushed her cheek with his knuckles.

Mistake. Her knees were already weak, and that was almost enough to send her tumbling head-first downstairs. She swayed, and he grabbed her and tucked her firmly into his side, then walked her downstairs, his hard, lean hip bumping into her softer one with every step, until by the time they reached the bottom she was ready to scream with—

What? Frustration? Longing?

Disappointment?

He let her go, and she followed him into the kitchen and sank gratefully into a chair. The children were nowhere to be seen, and he explained he'd sent them over to the café for lunch.

'Do you want to join them, or can you make do with bread and cheese and my company?'

Cheese gave her indigestion, but she wouldn't pass up on the offer of his company for the world.

'Oh, I guess I can make do,' she said softly, and he met her eyes and smiled, and her heart sank.

She'd known all along that she was in hot water. It was only then that she realised just how deep it was.

CHAPTER SEVEN

SHE needn't have worried.

After that morning, and once he was satisfied that his mother was looking after Izzy properly, Will avoided her whenever possible.

Whether he was avoiding her or simply getting on with his work she wasn't sure, but he was never around, and Izzy took to spending several hours at a time curled up on the sofa in the kitchen, with a cat on her lap and a book taken from the selection in the study.

She needed to rest, not only to get over the anaesthetic but because her sleep pattern was shot to blazes by the awkwardness of the cast and the pain in her arm, but the enforced holiday was anathema to her.

When the inactivity got too much, she went over to the café and sat in the corner, people-watching and chatting to Mrs T when she could spare the time. She couldn't help much, of course, because there was little that could be done one-handed, but if she could do anything she did, and if it got busy she took herself off for a little walk to get out of the way.

And she spoke to Kate, of course, on a daily basis, and went to the hospital in a taxi for her check-up at the fracture clinic, and went to physio, and by the end of the weekend she was tearing her hair out.

'Is your arm sore?' Rebecca asked on Sunday evening.

She looked at the little girl, so like her father that it hurt, and summoned up a smile.

'A bit. Why?'

'Because you're crabby. Mummy was always crabby when she was sore.'

A huge wave of guilt washed over Izzy, and she sat down at the table next to her and gave a wry grin. 'I'm sorry. I'm just feeling a bit trapped and bored.'

'Like wet play,' the child said sagely. 'I hate wet play. We have to stay inside and read or something, and the boys get horrible, and then the teachers get mad with us.'

'You ought to go out with Dad round the farm,' Michael said, wandering in on the tail-end of the conversation and dropping into the chair opposite. 'He likes company. He gets bored on his own, too. Dad, Izzy's bored. You need to take her round the farm with you.'

Izzy's head whipped round. She hadn't realised Will was there, too. How much had he heard, and how ungrateful would he think she was?

She dredged up an apologetic smile. 'I'm sorry. I'm just not used to doing nothing. I don't make a very good patient. I should go back to London, really.'

He looked puzzled. 'And do what?'

She shrugged. 'I could go into the office.'

'Is there anything going on at the moment that only you can do?'

She thought about it for a moment, and was a little shocked to realise that, no, there was nothing that would grind to a halt without her. The only thing she could be doing—would be doing—was drumming up more business, and they frankly didn't need it.

'No,' she replied. 'They can manage without me, I'm sure. Probably glad to be shot of me.'

His mouth twitched into a smile. 'So relax. How are you sleeping?'

She rolled her eyes. 'Not wonderfully well. I wake up early, when the painkillers wear off, and can't get back to sleep again. I'm usually awake when you get up.'

'So come down and have tea with me, and if you feel really energetic you can come out when I feed the stock and let the hens out and milk the cow. Nothing exciting, but it might beat lying in bed bored and hurting.'

It certainly would, for a whole raft of reasons she didn't really want to go into, either with Will or in front of his children, and none of them was anything to do with boredom or pain!

'I'm moving the sheep tomorrow,' he told her. 'The kids will be back at school, so I'll have to get them up and out in time for the bus, but after that I'll be putting the ewes and lambs into the trailer in batches and shipping them over there. You're welcome to join me.'

And so she found herself up at five-thirty the next day, sipping tea while the painkillers kicked in, walking round the yard with Will and watching as he checked the animals, scrubbed out water troughs, mixed feed, forked silage and all the other innumerable things that seemed to be necessary so horribly early in the morning.

Then she sat on a straw bale and watched as he hand-milked Bluebell, the house cow, and the gentle rhythmic slosh of the milk into the bucket nearly sent her to sleep.

It was hardly even light, and yet he'd done half a day's work, and she knew he didn't come upstairs to bed until at least eleven, if not later, shut away in his study battling with the paperwork that she knew he hated.

She was always in her room before he came up, because the pain in her arm was tiring and she was ready to escape from it by nine-thirty or so. She always saved her strongest painkillers for the night, and although she was worried they might be addictive, she thought the most addictive thing about them was the blissful oblivion they brought.

There was no way Will would need anything to bring him oblivion, she thought. No wonder he'd struck her as tired when she'd first seen him at the party the other week. He must be exhausted, and she wondered how on earth he kept going. Will-power and grim determination, most probably, and her lying around all day with a book and a sour expression was probably the last thing he needed.

The milking finished, they went back in and had breakfast with the children. She sat nursing a cup of tea while Will chivvied and coaxed them out of the door with their packed lunches and bags and PE kit, and then, while he made a few phone calls and in an effort to give something back for all his kindness, she loaded the dishwasher one-handed and put it on, then tried to sweep the kitchen floor.

Difficult, with Banjo barking and bouncing round biting the end of the broom and turning the whole procedure into an enormous and very noisy game.

'Banjo, stop it!' she said, laughing helplessly at the dog as his tail lashed and his eyes sparkled with mischief, and when he let go to bark she made a quick swipe for the crumbs under the table. Not quick enough. He seized it again and she shook her head and gave up.

Her hair was sliding out of its band, and she lifted her cast to brush it out of her way and caught sight of Will, standing in the doorway with a curious expression on her face, watching her intently.

Slowly she straightened, the dog and his game forgotten, conscious only of her wildly misbehaving hair and the hectic colour she could feel in her cheeks.

'What is it?' she said, her voice sounding strange to her ears, and he shrugged away from the doorframe and came over to her, taking the brush from her hand.

'Banjo, in your bed,' he said quietly, and the dog turned and walked reluctantly out to the utility room and flopped down with a grunt. Will propped the brush up against the wall, eased the band out of her hair and ordered her to sit. She felt his fingers against her nape and a shiver of something indefinable ran over her skin.

'What are you doing?'

'I was going to brush it.'

'You'll never get a brush through it. It needs a wash, but I can't manage. I can only just about cope with the shower. Your mother helped me with it last week, but it needs doing again desperately and I don't like to ask her. She's so busy.'

'I'll do it for you later,' he promised, and with gentle fingers he drew it back and secured it once more in the band. Then he stepped back, and she had an odd feeling that he was distancing himself from her. It felt curiously lonely.

'I'm going to do the sheep. Still want to come?'

She nodded, and felt her hair trying to escape again. Oh, well, there was nothing she could do about it. Maybe she should have it cut—or get Kate to send her hair straighteners on. In fact, there were so many things she was going to need if she was staying here that it would be impractical to ask Kate to deal with it.

'I'm going to have to go back to London,' she told him, and a quick frown flitted across his face and was gone.

'I thought we sorted that one out yesterday?'

She nodded. 'Yes—but there are things I need if I'm going to stay. I'll have to go back and get them. I can get a minicab to take me.'

The frown was back in force. 'Don't be silly. If you need to go, I'll take you.'

'But you can't! You're busy.'

'No. The weekends are impossible, but I can get cover during the week,' he told her. 'Once the lambs are out at pasture I can get Tim to do most of the work, and my father's always willing to pitch in with enough notice. It won't be a problem. Just give me a couple of days' notice.'

'Wednesday, then?' she said with a wry smile, and he gave a grunt of laughter.

'Take me literally! But Wednesday will be fine. I'll sort it out.'

'I'll ring Kate later—get her primed. I'll need to go in and do one or two things in the office.'

'Fine.' He looked up at the clock. 'Right—we need to move the sheep. You up for it?'

'Just call me Bo Peep,' she said with a grin, and he laughed and squeezed her shoulder briefly before heading for the door.

He kitted her out with boots—his mother's, he said, to her relief—and a thick jumper she'd seen him wear, because although the sun was shining it was only April still, and he'd warned her it could be cold down on the salt marshes at the far side of the farm.

She was glad of it. It took hours, and she saw Banjo's ability to round up the kitchen broom put to good use.

'So he's not just a pretty face,' she said to Will, and he chuckled.

'He's all right. He's young, and a bit too enthusiastic, but he's a good boy, really. He'll be a good sheepdog when he's settled down a bit.'

She thought he seemed pretty darned good now, but what did she know? She just trailed along, keeping Will company and trying not to get too sidetracked by the sight of his muscles rippling as he caught an escaping ewe and manhandled her into the trailer, or picked up a big metal hurdle and swung it round to create a funnel to drive the sheep towards the trailer.

Eye candy. That was what the Americans called it.

She sighed quietly. She might as well enjoy the view. She'd never get close enough to touch.

'How on earth do you get a comb through it?'

'Slowly and carefully and bit by bit,' Izzy replied,

and he stared down at the tangled mess in his hands and sighed.

'Well, I'll try,' he said, not willing to promise anything, and she sat at his feet on the rug in the kitchen, with him on the sofa behind her, his knees bracketing her shoulders and the heat from her body searing him through the fabric of his jeans, and slowly, inch by inch, he worked his way over her hair and turned it from wire wool to smooth, shining wet tresses that lay heavily in his hands.

'Now what?'

She shrugged. 'Don't know. I always put something on it to help style it, either to straighten it or to let the curl out. I don't have anything with me. Try finger-scrunching it.'

He tipped her head back with a blunt finger and brought his head down beside hers so she didn't have to dislocate her neck to see him. 'Finger-scrunching?' he said, a trifle desperately.

'You know, sort of cobble it up in your hands and put the bounce back.'

He gave a strangled laugh. 'I've just spent nearly an hour getting the bounce out of it!' he protested, but nevertheless he tried, and, sure enough, it started to dry with curl rather than frizz. Probably because he'd put half a bottle of conditioner on it to try and settle it down, but now it was drying, and it had shine and bounce and curl, and he sifted his fingers slowly through it over and over again, feeling the weight and texture of it, enjoying the quiet moment with her.

Dragging it out, in fact, because it was the only feeble excuse he had to touch her, and he'd been aching to touch her for days now.

Weeks.

Hell, years. Twelve long, agonising years.

'Ouch!'

'Sorry.'

He disentangled his finger from the rebellious strand that had caught it. 'I think that's all I can do,' he said, and, standing up, he stepped round her and went out into the study, leaving her sitting on the floor staring after him and wondering, probably, what on earth she'd done wrong.

Nothing. Nothing, that was, short of looking too damn beautiful for her own good, and smelling of soap and shampoo and warm, desirable woman.

'I'm going to tackle some paperwork,' he growled, and shut the study door behind himself with a defiant little bang.

Izzy stared at the door for several long seconds. Well. So much for thinking they were having a relaxing, intimate little interlude.

He'd dried her hair, and now it was dry he'd gone. Job done.

She pulled a face, her mouth tucking in at one side ruefully. One step forward, half a mile back. He hadn't been slamming doors this morning.

Oh, well. He was taking her back to London on Wednesday, and if he was as grumpy as this on the way there, she might not bother to come back.

He wasn't grumpy. He was friendly enough, but a little distant, and she thought it would have been easier with a minicab driver. At least she wouldn't have felt obliged to entertain him or worry about his mental health!

They went straight to her apartment, taking the lift up from the underground car park. She'd thought she'd have to bribe the man on the barrier to let them in, but one look at her arm and he agreed they could use one of the empty slots.

'Hussein's away. You can have his space. As it's you, Miss Brooke,' he said, and eyed Will with undisguised curiosity.

She could have done without that, but it was too late now. A cab with a plate on, of course, would have occasioned no comment whatsoever, but Will's elderly Land Rover Discovery, with mud up to the window line, was a bit of a giveaway.

Her apartment looked as if she'd never been away. More correctly, she thought, looking at it in dismay, it looked as if she'd never lived there—as if no one lived there. Where were the personal touches? The piles of books, the clutter of photo frames, the school bag slung in the corner with its contents spilling out?

She even missed the smell of wet dog.

'I need to change out of these things, and I'd better do something with my hair—spray something in it to tame it again. Can you give me a hand to do that in a minute?'

'Sure,' Will said. 'Holler when you need me.' He let himself out onto the roof garden and went over to the railing, leaning on it and staring out across the river with a strange look on his face.

Izzy didn't have the mental energy to work out what

was wrong with him. He was such a complex man, with so many layers, she was discovering, that she had no idea where to start. Had he always been so private, so withdrawn?

No. That had happened some time in the past twelve years, since he'd left her. Probably since Julia's illness. Many people withdrew when they lost a loved one. He might even have depression as a result.

What a curious thought.

She went into her bedroom and opened her wardrobe, and was faced with row upon row of business suits, blouses, skirts, smart trousers, endless high-heeled shoes and boots and strappy sandals. She wouldn't need them on the farm!

She turned instead to her gym kit, and found what she was looking for. Jog bottoms—ones that fitted her, rather than Michael, although she'd been very grateful for them—and wide-sleeved tops that would go over her cast.

She dug out a pair of jeans and some trainers with Velcro, because she'd been wearing a pair of Michael's trainers for the past week, and they were a touch on the small side as well as having laces which she had to have help with.

Then, just out of vanity and to counteract the hugely unsexy outer layers, she opened her underwear drawer and hooked out a heap of froth. Pretty lace, slippery silk, warm to the touch and soft to the skin, gleaming satin and fine, transparent mesh. Nothing weighed more than a few grams, and it would make her feel better.

And her hair straighteners. She threw them on the

pile, although she couldn't use them one-handed, but maybe she could talk Rebecca into helping her.

She gave the door a dubious look, but there was no way Will would come in unless she called him. She stripped off her clothes with difficulty, although she was getting better at it, and went into her bathroom. She couldn't use the power shower, but the hand-held spray over the bath might be quite useful.

She washed herself as thoroughly as she could without soaking the cast, then dried and put on her own deodorant, her own moisturiser, her own perfume—it was wonderful. She started to feel human again, and she was just humming gently as she put the finishing touches to her make-up when there was a tap on the door.

'Just a minute,' she called, and picked up the towel. 'OK.'

He came in and hesitated, his eyes raking over her, and then he closed them and let out a ragged sigh. 'Izzy, for God's sake,' he groaned. 'Give a man a break and cover yourself up.'

And then she realised with dismay that she was standing in front of the mirrored wall behind the basin, and although she was holding the towel up in front, there was nothing behind her but the lingering mist from her shower to keep her from his eyes.

'I'm sorry,' she muttered, flustered now, and went out into the bedroom and reached for the pile of underwear. She picked up the first pair of knickers she found, if you could call them that. A thong, the briefest briefs in all the world, designed to wear under a lace dress and be invisible.

Oh, well. She pulled them on one-handed, muttering at the elastic which managed to twist as she pulled them up, and then she was dragging on her jeans and the loose cotton top that she'd found which would hopefully go over the cast.

But, of course, she couldn't do up the jeans one-handed, especially not since Mrs T's cooking, and with a sigh of exasperation she turned to Will.

'OK, you can open your eyes now. Can you help me with the zip, please?'

He looked down at the yawning vee in the front of her jeans, the skin behind so slightly covered by the fine mesh and lace of her invisible underwear, and his mouth tightened.

He's angry, she thought, but his hands were gentle. He drew the edges of her waistband together, fastened the stud and slid up the zip without comment, then stepped back out of range.

'Is this what you're taking?' he asked, looking at the bed.

She was sitting on the edge of the bed, shoving her feet into the trainers, and she glanced over her shoulder at the heap of clothes. 'Yes. There's a soft bag in the bottom of the wardrobe at that end. They should all fit in there.'

He produced it, his fingers automatically caressing the butter-soft brown leather, and she remembered how tactile he'd always been, how sensitive to texture. Was that still true, with his hands so callused from working on the farm? Or was the pleasure of touch now lost to him?

How sad that would be, she thought.

He held the bag open with one hand and stuffed the clothes in with the other, handling her underwear as if it contained live snakes. She suppressed the urge to laugh, but then he looked up and his face was tautly controlled, and she felt the laughter drain away. He probably thought she was hopelessly frivolous and impractical.

'That everything?' he asked, and she nodded.

'My wash things are ready, on the side in the bathroom. I'll get them.'

She went round him, careful to give him a wide berth, and retrieved her toiletries from the shelf. They slotted neatly into another little bag made for the purpose, and then she truly was ready.

'Nothing else?'

She shook her head. 'I don't think so. Do you think I've forgotten anything?'

'Nightclothes?'

She shrugged. 'I thought I'd carry on sleeping in a T-shirt. It's easy.'

He growled something under his breath and hoisted the bags into one hand. 'Right. Let's go.'

He left her to follow him, and she caught up with him in the big open living room.

'Do you want a drink before we go, or shall we get something downstairs?'

'What about going to the office?'

She shrugged again. 'I thought we could do that after lunch, if you're not in a hurry, but since you obviously are we can go now. We'll grab something to eat on the way home.'

She pressed the button to close the roof garden door,

then found her lift pass and opened the door with a smile. 'Shall we go?'

Definitely should have come in a minicab, she thought as they threaded their way through the traffic. He got lost once, because she was distracted, and had to go a longer way round. It didn't matter, really, but it obviously irritated him, and she was getting ready to tell him to go back alone when they arrived at the office.

There was no problem with parking there, of course. They went straight into her space, since her car was at her apartment, where she kept it, and up in the lift to her office to be greeted with delight and concern by Kate.

'How long are you going to be?' Will asked when the kerfuffle had died down a little and everyone had exclaimed over the cast and tutted at the bags under her eyes.

'Not long. Why? Did you want to do something?'

It was his turn to shrug. 'Thought I might take a stroll—too much sitting about.'

'Give me an hour,' she said, and he nodded and went back out to the lifts, leaving her at Kate's mercy.

Kate took her by the arm and all but towed her into her office. 'How *are* you? It's really good to see you again—I've been so worried. How does it feel?'

Izzy scowled at her hand and flexed her sore, swollen fingers in disgust. 'Not wonderful. It keeps me awake at night.'

'Sure it's not him?' Kate teased, and Izzy felt her colour rise.

'Don't be ridiculous. Didn't you see how impatient

he was? He's a reluctant hero if ever I met one. I think he's feeling a bit trapped by his better nature at the moment, so we'd better not take too long. What's been happening?'

Kate rolled her eyes. 'Where do you want me to start? I've had Daniel O'Keeffe on the phone at least twice a day, begging you to go back. I've explained you've broken your arm, and anyway you aren't interested, but the man seems to have gone deaf. And Steve is driving me crazy. He wants you, Izzy, and you're going to have to tell him to take a hike. I can't, and he's pestering me for your landline number. I told him I don't know it and your mobile's broken.'

'Oh, damn, I forgot the charger,' she said. 'We're going to have to go back to my place.' She thought of Will's reluctance to spend any more time in there, but it was too bad. She needed her phone, she needed her independence, and she needed—

She needed to be back here, with her arm working and her freedom back, she thought, but it was curiously unappealing. Out of the blue she had a much better idea, and it didn't necessarily involve Will at all.

'How do you fancy closing the office and having a few weeks off, Kate? We can leave Ally to tell everyone that we're on annual shutdown, or something, and we can keep in touch with the employment agency staff and make sure there aren't any problems. It's years since we played hooky. I reckon it's time.'

Kate's jaw dropped. 'Close the office?' she squeaked, and opened and shut her mouth a few more times without saying anything at all apart from 'But—!' and 'I mean…' and things like that.

Izzy grinned at her. 'I take it that's a yes?'

'Oh, yes! Oh, boy, is it a yes! And you know what? I'm going to go to Australia to see my mother. I haven't seen her for two years, and she keeps nagging. Izzy, I love you!'

She hugged her, suddenly remembering her arm when the cast caught them both in the ribs, and then she stood back and looked long and hard at Izzy.

'Will you be all right? Truly? He looked a bit cross.'

'Will?' She shrugged. 'He's just in a bit of a grump for some reason. I may not include him in my plans. I mean, he's been very kind to me, but he obviously doesn't want me around. I'll go away somewhere—lie in the sun somewhere exotic and read trashy novels and drink blue cocktails and fend off the press. I might even find a man to rub in my sunscreen,' she joked.

Then she noticed a fleeting panic on Kate's face and turned to see Will standing in the doorway, his eyes curiously expressionless.

'I did knock,' he said. 'You didn't hear me. I'm ready when you are.'

And he turned on his heel and walked out.

'Oops,' she said softly, wondering just how much he'd heard. 'Better go. I'll leave you to tell everyone about the office—keep them all on full pay, and tell them we'll be back on the first of June. Dream up something appropriate for the answer-machine so Ally doesn't have to deal with all the calls for this office as well as the other one. You'd better tell her to contact me on my mobile, initially, until I know where I'll be. And have fun, and thank you for everything.'

She kissed Kate's cheek and hugged her briefly, then went out into the reception area.

Will was standing there staring out of the window again, and she smiled at him brightly. 'All set,' she said, and he nodded curtly and headed towards the lift.

Oh, rats. Whatever he'd heard hadn't improved his mood at all, she realised, and could have kicked herself for making that stupid crack about finding a man. Nothing could have been further from her thoughts, and the idea that he would now think that of her was curiously painful.

Still, trying to explain would only make the hole deeper. The only thing to do was to stop digging, and so she followed him in silence, suddenly aware of the unfamiliar sensation of butterflies dancing madly in her insides.

CHAPTER EIGHT

HE WAS silent in the lift, all the way down to the car park level, then helped her into his car and edged out into the traffic without a word.

'I need to go back to my apartment,' she told him. 'I've forgotten my phone charger.'

Did he sigh? If he did, it was under his breath, but it was irrelevant. She was well aware of the fact that he was less than happy. What she didn't know was why, but it didn't matter. She'd be out of his hair soon. She had a check-up at the hospital on Friday, and after that she'd go away and leave him in peace. She couldn't see him complaining.

'Have you had anything to eat or drink yet?' she asked, hoping he'd say no so she could suggest popping into the café in her apartment block, but he nodded.

'I grabbed a coffee and a roll round the corner,' he said, and fell back into silence.

So much for that idea, then.

They turned into the underground parking lane and were waved through with a broad smile. The lift whisked them silently up to her apartment, and she left him hovering in the living room while she went into the bedroom to pick up her phone charger.

It was plugged in, of course, down behind the bedside cabinet, where she could only reach it with her left arm. Her right just couldn't get round the corner, and there was no way she had the strength in her left hand even to flick the switch, far less pull the plug out of the wall.

And that meant asking Will.

She went back out and found him on the roof terrace again, staring blindly out over the horizon, his face forbidding.

'Will?'

He turned, and for a second there was a raw pain in his eyes that took her breath away. Then it was gone, replaced by a half-smile that barely touched his mouth. 'What is it?'

The pain had shocked her, and for a second she couldn't think straight. 'Um—I can't unplug the phone charger. It's behind the bedside table and I can't reach with my right hand.'

Was that alarm that flickered in his eyes? Surely not. Had he really been so embarrassed by the incident earlier that he was worried about being in her bedroom? How silly. He hadn't shown any sign of worrying in her bedroom in his house, so why here? It wasn't as if he'd seen anything he hadn't seen before, after all.

And what had that pain been about? He must have been thinking about Julia, missing her, desperate to get Izzy out of his life so he could go back to grieving alone. Oh, damn. And she was making it so much harder for him.

He followed her back to her room and hunkered down by the bedside cabinet, pulling out the plug and coiling up the flex without a word.

'Thank you.'

He didn't even look at her. 'Right, is there anything else, or can we get the hell out of here now?' he asked bluntly, and the shock of it brought her to her senses.

She'd had enough. She'd loved him, for heaven's sake. He'd loved her. She was the injured party in all this, and there was no justification for giving her the cold shoulder. If he didn't want her staying with him, all he had to do was say so, not just freeze her out.

'You didn't have to be here,' she reminded him just as bluntly. 'I suggested a minicab. This was your idea.'

'Well, it was a lousy one,' he growled.

That was it. She tipped her head on one side, put her hands on her hips and glared at him. 'Have I done something specific to make you hate me, or is it just habit?' she asked without preamble.

His hands stilled, and then he rose slowly to his full height, the charger dangling forgotten from his fingers.

'What makes you think I hate you?' he asked, his voice incredulous.

She laughed shortly. 'The fact that you've hardly spoken a word to me all day? The fact that you can't seem to stand to look at me? You *asked* me to stay, Will. It wasn't my idea—but you don't have to worry. I'm leaving, just as soon as I've had my check-up on Friday—maybe even before then.'

'And going on holiday somewhere exotic to drink cocktails with some man you've picked up on the beach—what's the matter, Izzy?' he said bitterly. 'That door not revolving fast enough for you these days?' He gave her bedroom door a pointed look, and she stared at him in astonishment.

'You bastard,' she said slowly. 'You know that's just empty rumour.'

'Do I?' He gave a hollow, strangled laugh and rammed one hand through his hair. 'I'm not sure I know anything any more, except that this is tearing me apart. You really think I can't stand to be around you? I must be a better actor than I thought.'

The anger drained out of her, and the butterflies started up again in earnest. 'I don't understand,' she said unsteadily.

He put the phone charger down and moved towards her, slowly but surely. 'Don't you? Look at me, Izzy. Really look at me. What do you see?'

She looked, and her breath jammed in her throat.

Hunger. Dear God. Raw, elemental hunger—a hunger so great it should have terrified her. It didn't. It was her own hunger that did that—hunger for a man who'd already told her there was no future for them. Hunger for a man she hadn't forgotten in twelve years, and never would.

She lifted her hand towards him, then it fell to her side.

'Can you see it, Izzy?' he asked softly, his voice changed almost beyond recognition. 'How much I need you? You see, the simple truth is I can hardly keep my hands off you. Helping you, having you around for the last few days and having to do things for you—that's been bad enough. Drying your hair the other night was torture—and coming in here earlier and seeing you wearing little more than your cast and a squirt of perfume—I nearly lost it, Izzy. And I'm going to lose it now if we don't get out of here soon.'

The butterflies disappeared, banished at a stroke by his words. He wasn't angry with her. He didn't hate her. He wanted her—wanted her, for heaven's sake! She nearly laughed aloud with relief.

Instead she lifted her hand again, and this time she slid it gently but firmly round the back of his neck and drew him down to meet her mouth.

'So lose it, Will,' she said softly. 'Lose it with me.'

He sucked in his breath sharply, but then let it out on a ragged sigh and lifted his head. 'I can't—we can't. Not unless you're on the Pill or whatever.'

She dropped her head forwards against his chest and let out a groan of frustration. 'I'm not. Why would I be? I don't do this, Will. Ever—despite what the gossips say.'

He stepped back. 'Then let's get out of here—now, while we still can.'

But she didn't want to. She shook her head and smiled. 'No. Wait. I've got an idea. There's a machine in the gym.'

She backed away from him, then turned and ran out of her apartment, grabbing her bag and her key on the way. She went down in the lift to the gym, and as luck would have it bumped straight into Freddie.

'Iz—hey, what have you done?'

'Broken my arm. Sorry. Won't be in for a while. I've just come to see if I left something in the changing rooms,' she ad-libbed. 'Sorry, Freddie, got to fly. I'm going up to Suffolk in a minute. I'll see you when I'm back.'

And she shot into the changing room with a sigh of relief, then rummaged in her purse for money.

Amazingly she had the right change, and there was no one about. She shoved the money in the slot, pulled open the drawer with shaking fingers and reached in just as a voice called her name.

Damn. Of all the times—!

'Izzy! How are you? Haven't seen you for ages!'

'Oh, hi, Maggie,' she said, slamming the drawer shut and dropping the condoms into her bag. 'I'm fine.'

Maggie's eyes went from the dispenser to Izzy and her brows arched as her smile widened. 'Yes, I can see that. Well, well.'

Inspiration struck. Izzy looked at the dispenser, smacked her forehead with her palm and laughed. 'What an idiot! I've used the wrong machine—I wanted tampons! Oh, rats.'

She rummaged again for change, but then didn't have enough, and Maggie kindly lent her some.

'Thanks. You're a star. Sorry, got to go—personal emergency!' she said breathlessly, and all but ran out. She made it back to the apartment without bumping into anyone else, and went back into the bedroom on a bubble of laughter.

'You won't believe it—'

Will wasn't there. He wasn't in the living room, either, and panic started to rise in her chest—and then she heard the shower running. Her heart slowed and she closed her eyes. Thank God. For a horrible moment—

She went back into the bedroom and perched on the end of the bed, kicked off her trainers and waited. Moments later he emerged, a towel tied round his waist, his hair roughly dried and dripping rivulets down over his broad, solid chest.

'Any joy?'

She waggled the packet at him, and his shoulders dropped about three inches. His sigh of relief was heartfelt, and with a laugh she went into his arms.

This was Will—the Will she'd fallen in love with when she'd been just a girl on the brink of womanhood.

He'd been little more than a boy then, but not now. Now he was most emphatically a man, and for all the burning hunger that blazed in his eyes he didn't seem in any hurry. He lowered his head slowly and brushed her lips with his once, twice, before he settled his mouth over hers and kissed her thoroughly.

He didn't touch her elsewhere, except to steady her shoulders with his strong, hard hands, and the urgency went out of her.

He was right. They'd waited twelve years for this. There was no hurry now. She gave herself up to sensation...

She was beautiful.

He propped himself up on one elbow and waited patiently for her to wake. There was no rush. He was enjoying the view—not the glorious panorama of the river through the window, but the lush, tender curves and softly shadowed hollows of her body. He felt his own stirring again, and smiled sadly.

To think he'd imagined he was strong enough to walk away from this again.

He'd done it once, and it had been the hardest thing

he'd ever done in his life. He couldn't do it again, and yet he knew it would come to that.

Whatever. He'd take what he could get, and deal with the other later.

He trailed a finger up the underside of her arm, flung above her head like a sleeping child. Yet she was no child, this woman who'd taken him into her body with such tenderness and rapture. He felt his heart contract. There was so much she didn't know, so much he should have told her.

But there was time. He'd tell her when she woke.

Leaning forwards, he pressed his lips to the soft, cool skin of her midriff. She stirred, murmuring his name sleepily, and he moved up, trailing his tongue over her nipple and blowing over the damp skin. It puckered, and her eyes fluttered open, soft and unfocused.

'Well, hello there,' he murmured, his mouth kicking up in an involuntary smile.

Her mouth curved in answer, and she lifted herself on her right elbow and kissed his lips. He toyed with her mouth, savouring the moment, then lifted his head, staring down at her in wonder.

'We need to talk,' he said softly.

She lay back against the pillows. 'No.'

'Yes. There are things you need to know—about me and Julia—'

'No.' She put her finger on his lips, silencing him. 'No, Will. Please. It's over—in the past. I don't want to know. It doesn't matter any more. All that matters is this—what we are to each other now. Please—just give me this.'

He couldn't argue—not when her eyes were still

glazed from their loving. With a quiet sigh he drew her gently into his arms and covered her mouth with his.

The journey home—odd how she thought of it as home—was nothing like their journey into London that morning.

They didn't talk much this time, either, at least at first, but their silence was one of contentment. They didn't need to talk. Their bodies had said all there was to say, and for a large part of the journey their hands lay linked together between them, his fingers idly caressing hers as he drove one-handed up the A12.

The traffic was reasonably light at that time of the evening, and there was no hurry. He'd phoned his parents earlier, and asked if they could watch over the children and make sure the stock were all OK, and they'd been all right about it, he said.

Izzy looked across at him now, the strong planes of his face visible intermittently in the headlights of oncoming cars.

'OK?' she asked, and he threw her a smile.

'Never better. You?'

Her smile grew wider. 'Me too. How long till we're there?'

He shrugged. 'Half an hour? Three-quarters, maybe?'

'What about the children? Are they at your parents' house or yours?'

'Ours,' he said, and for a moment she thought he was referring to them as a couple. Then she realised he was talking about him and the children—his im-

mediate family, to which, of course she didn't belong.
It was a sobering thought.

'I would have thought your mother would want to
be in her own home,' she said, and he gave her a
slightly crooked smile.

'Well, it is, in a way. Was for years. And it's easier
during term-time to get the kids settled in their own
beds and make sure their homework's done. They'll
use any excuse to fail to do it.'

Izzy tried to imagine babysitting her grandchildren
at some point in the future and couldn't. It was too far
removed from everything that was familiar to her, and
she wasn't sure she'd know where to begin. 'Won't
she be bored?'

He laughed. 'Not a chance. She's doing a bit of baking, but she's had to bring everything with her. She
wanted to try out some recipes and she needs all her
strange ingredients. I don't tend to have a lot in the
house.'

Izzy chuckled. 'She mentioned that,' she said, and
then she wondered what Mrs T was thinking about their
delayed return. 'When you asked her to babysit—what
did you tell her?' she asked him thoughtfully.

He shrugged. 'Oh—just that you'd had more to do
in the office than you'd anticipated, and that we were
hungry and we'd decided to stop to eat and give the
traffic time to die down.'

'The truth, then,' she teased with a smile, and he
laughed.

'You want me to tell her the truth?'

She thought of their wild and passionate lovemaking
and felt her colour rise. 'Good grief, no!' she said

firmly. 'Anything but! On a need-to-know basis, your mother doesn't.'

'Well, at least we agree about that. In fact, since we're on the subject, we could do with some ground rules here, Izzy.'

Ground rules? A line drawn in the sand that she wouldn't overstep? She was hurt that he should consider it necessary to mention it, and so her tone was sharper than it might have been. 'Let me guess—no sex in the house, no cuddling in front of the children, no talking dirty in the utility room when we think the kids are out of earshot—what kind of an idiot do you think I am, Will?'

He had the grace to look embarrassed. 'I'm sorry, but—they're my kids, Izzy. They've been through a lot. This is their mother we're talking about.'

Actually, she'd thought they were talking about themselves, but apparently not. She sighed deeply and rubbed her good hand over her face. 'I'm sorry, too. I didn't mean to snap. Of course we don't want to do anything to draw attention to our relationship, either in front of the children or anyone else, for that matter. I've had enough attention from the media about affairs I *haven't* had without drawing their attention to one I am háving.'

He looked slightly startled. 'Media?' he said, as if the thought hadn't even occurred to him. But why should it? He didn't live in the glare of publicity like she did.

'That's why I don't like eating out anywhere except the apartment block, or very occasionally that wine bar if it's quiet,' she explained. 'I should be safe up here, because the local press aren't looking for me. I'm not nearly as interesting as an oil spill in the North Sea or a thatched cottage on fire. I'm sure they won't bother with me if I keep my head down, but if I start making waves—well, they'll have a field-day, and you'll be the ones to suffer.'

His mouth tightened. 'So let's not do anything to provoke it. I don't want the kids involved in anything sordid like that.'

'And I do?' she said, piqued again. 'Don't worry, Will. Like I said, *I* won't be doing anything to attract attention.'

They fell silent again, but this time it wasn't a comfortable silence. Their conversation had simply served to underline the huge gulf between them. For a short while Izzy had allowed herself to believe that everything would be all right, but now she could see that she'd been wildly optimistic.

It was an affair—that was all. Nothing more, nothing less, and there was no point in trying to talk it up to herself. She was his house-guest, an old flame, and a willing one at that. They had been thrown together, and only a fool or a saint would turn down an opportunity like that.

And Will Thompson had never been either.

Will was finding it increasingly difficult to stick to those stupid ground rules. He was up at five-thirty, and sometimes Izzy came down to the kitchen with him, warm and tousled from sleep, and the urge to drag her straight back up the stairs and into his bed was practically overwhelming.

So he'd growl at her, and then he'd feel her withdrawing from him, and he'd want to kick himself for being so insensitive. Or over-sensitive, more like—over-sensitive to her presence, her wide-open smile and the promise in her eyes.

He ached for her with a physical pain, and working himself to death was the only way round it. So he worked. He shifted the muck heap, a messy job he'd been meaning to do for ages, and relocated the chickens onto fresh ground, and tore the roof off the old cow barn and replaced it—all on top of his normal hectic workload—just so he didn't have the time or the energy to think about her.

It was a week before she pulled him up on it.

He was in the study, struggling with the endless paperwork and hardly able to keep his eyes open, and she came in, dressed in a pair of loose pyjama trousers and a baggy T-shirt, and perched on the edge of his desk, right in his way.

'We need to talk,' she said firmly, and he slammed down the pen and glared up at her.

'No. We need to make love,' he said, and the expressions chasing across her face would have made him laugh if he hadn't been so desperate.

And then she smiled. 'I agree. But when? And where? You haven't sat down in the last week—you've hardly paused long enough to swallow your food. Your children don't recognise you any more—do you know how much time I've spent with them in the evenings?'

Guilt washed over him, and he scrubbed his face with his hands and pressed his fingertips into his tired, tired eyes.

'Izzy, I'm sorry,' he said gruffly. 'I didn't mean to do that to you—I just wasn't thinking. I was trying not to, in fact. You're driving me crazy.'

She bent over and pressed her lips to his. 'Shh. Don't worry. What are you doing tomorrow?'

'Tomorrow?' He felt his body stir with reaction. 'I don't know. You tell me—you've obviously got something up your sleeve.'

'I'd like to visit the lambs with you, and take a picnic, and go down to the river and have lunch. We could spread a blanket out under the trees—'

'And make love in broad daylight? Are you crazy?' He laughed, his bottom lip caught between his teeth, the idea hideously appealing. That was where he'd kissed her the first time, where it had all started, and he only had to think about it and he needed her. 'Hell, Izzy, don't do this to me.'

'We could just spend time together—eat, rest a little. We don't have to—well, you know.'

'Yes, we do,' he said softly. 'I need to hold you so badly.'

'You can hold me. You can hold me now.'

He shook his head. 'The kids,' he said, conscious as ever of their presence just overhead. He couldn't do that to them—not with Izzy, who could never settle here with them and be part of a permanent family. If they walked in they'd start asking questions, and they'd be entitled to answers.

And he had none to give them that were even remotely suitable for their ears.

'A picnic?' he said, going back to Izzy's earlier suggestion, and she nodded.

'I thought I could get some things from the café during the morning and we could set off late morning. Do the lambs first—'

'No. We'll have lunch first, then check the lambs. If I'm going to get that close to you, I want a shower first.'

Probably a cold one.

He looked down at the desk and sighed. 'If you could just get that delectable bottom off my paperwork, I'll be able to finish off here and get some sleep, or I'll be dozing off in mid-picnic.'

She chuckled and stood up, turning to look down at the endless piles of stuff.

'Good grief,' she said weakly. 'What is this lot?'

He shrugged. 'Mostly dealt with but unfiled. There's all sorts of stuff that could be thrown out, I expect, but I don't know where to begin. Paperwork's not my thing.'

'But it is mine. Could I help you? Sort through it, try and make some sense of it? Have you got a filing cabinet?'

'Yeah—behind the door. It's virtually empty.'

She looked from the cabinet to the desk to him, and shook her head in mock despair. Or maybe not mock. He felt his mouth tighten.

'I'm sorry. It's not my strong point.'

'It isn't, is it? But don't worry, you have all sorts of other sterling qualities which more than make up for it. I'll have a look through it all tomorrow and see if I can tackle it. I might need your help for some of it.'

He snorted. 'I don't doubt it. My mother used to do it all, but she's too busy now, and anyway, it's all farm stuff and she's got enough to do with her own accounts and records.'

'I'll do it. Don't worry. Why don't you come up to bed now? You look shattered and it's after midnight already.'

'Come up to bed?' he said weakly. 'Hell, Izzy, you know how to push my buttons, don't you?'

She coloured softly. 'You know perfectly well what I mean,' she said, her brisk voice quite at odds with the warm blush on her cheeks and the sensual awareness lingering in those beautiful soft green eyes. 'I'm going up. I'll see you tomorrow.'

He pushed the chair back and drew her into his arms. 'I'm sorry—sorry it's so difficult, sorry I'm so tired, sorry I'm so crabby. How's your arm these days? I haven't even asked.'

Her smile was gentle and forgiving, and just made him feel worse. 'It's OK. Hurts a bit sometimes if I overdo it, but otherwise it's all right.'

He nodded, then, unable to help himself, he bent his head and kissed her. His hands slid down over her bottom, cupping the firm swell and easing her against him. Heat rocketed through him, and with a ragged groan he dragged his mouth away from hers and stepped back.

'Go on—go up. We'll continue this tomorrow.'

'I'll hold you to that,' she said softly, and her smile nearly had him reaching for her again. It would have done, if she hadn't slipped through the door and pulled it firmly closed behind her.

He sat down carefully at the desk, conscious only of

the tightness of his jeans and the promise of tomorrow. To hell with the paperwork. He couldn't concentrate.

Yanking the door open, he strode through to the kitchen, tugged on his coat, shoved his feet into his boots and did one final and quite unnecessary stock check.

Anything rather than stay in the house and listen to Izzy's bed creaking gently as she climbed back into it and snuggled down under the quilt alone.

'Tomorrow,' he told himself, and Banjo wagged his tail and grinned. He ruffled the dog's ears. 'You don't know the half of it, mate,' he said affectionately. 'Come on. Time for bed.'

And, please God, he'd have the self-control to walk upstairs past her door and keep on going.

CHAPTER NINE

Izzy couldn't believe it. He'd actually gone along with her plans for the picnic and not found some feeble excuse!

She hadn't really expected him to agree. He'd done everything in his power to keep out of her way since they'd come back from London, and she'd been starting to wonder if he was regretting making love to her. Talking to him last night, she'd decided that the only thing he was regretting was that they couldn't find the opportunity to do it again.

She'd spent the week wandering aimlessly about, chatting to Mrs T, reading and trying to keep out of his way. Emma had rescued her on Monday and taken her out for lunch, and they'd had a long chat which had done nothing more than underline for Izzy just how far removed her lifestyle was from that of all her old friends.

Emma had asked about Izzy's job, and looked stunned and dumbfounded when she'd explained what she actually did with her days.

'Good grief! I couldn't do that.'

'And I couldn't bring up three children.'

'How about two?' Emma asked, and Izzy just laughed at her friend's unsubtle fishing.

'I don't think so.'

'So—how are things with Will?' Emma asked, apparently changing the subject and yet not doing so at all, and Izzy just shook her head in apparent amusement and took the remark at face value.

'Will's fine, as far as I know,' she told her. 'To be honest, I hardly ever see him. He's so busy on the farm it's ridiculous, and he works in the office until after midnight.'

Emma tutted. 'He always looks exhausted. I used to think he was trying to get over Julia, but maybe it's just that there's too much to do and not enough people to do it.'

And, with that in mind, on the morning of the picnic Izzy went over to the café early to organise the food so she could go and make a start on the office as soon as it was all arranged.

'A picnic?' Mrs T exclaimed, and beamed hugely. 'What a wonderful idea! Oh, Izzy—now, what have we got? Pepper flan's on again, or there's a chicken and bacon tart, and I can always make you up some sandwiches. I know what Will likes—how about you? What should I put in for you?'

She shook her head, totally bemused by the choice. 'Everything looks wonderful,' she said, staring into the chiller. I can never decide. Just give us whatever you've got too much of.'

Mrs T clicked her tongue disapprovingly. 'Nonsense. You go. I'll find you something not too messy to eat that you can manage with one hand, and I'll put in a bottle of water and a flask of coffee. All right?'

'On one condition.'

'What's that?'

'This is my treat for him. I want you to let me pay for it.'

Mrs T looked at her sternly and drew herself up. 'You'll do no such thing. You're a guest here, and a very welcome one, and Will's my son. I wouldn't dream of charging either of you for any of it, and I'm insulted that you should find it necessary.'

Izzy closed her eyes and sighed. 'I'm sorry. I didn't mean to offend you, but I've been here day and night, abusing your hospitality—'

'Fiddlesticks. I'm not offended. I'm just not letting you pay. Go on, go and make yourself beautiful—not that that will take you long.'

Izzy laughed wryly. 'I don't know so much. My hair—'

'I'll come over and give you a hand with it again tonight,' she promised.

'Thanks. Right, I'd better go, I promised Will I'd have a look at the study for him and try and sort out that mountain of paper.'

'Good grief! Well, if you're going to tackle that lot I'd better put in a few extra calories and a dash of brain-food! I don't envy you, dear. I don't suppose you have the slightest idea what you've taken on.'

Oh, she did. Or she thought she did, until she went in there and started sifting through the piles. It seemed to fall into three groups—obvious rubbish, domestic paperwork and things related to the farm.

Rubbish first, she thought, and, retrieving a bin bag from the kitchen drawer, hung it over the front of one of the filing cabinet drawers and heaved all the junk mail, newspapers, three-year old telephone directories and the like into it.

That made a huge difference. Then she separated farm from home, and then subdivided home again, into things about school, utility bills and so on.

The farm would be harder, and she'd need to take advice on that, but by the time Will came in at twelve and stuck his head round the door a goodly portion of the massive oak desk was visible.

'Good grief!' He did a mild double-take and stared at her. 'Where did it all go?'

She pointed at the bin bag, and a look of panic so great it was almost comical crossed his face. 'It's all right. Anything I wasn't utterly sure of is still here on the desk.'

His shoulders dropped and he grinned faintly. 'OK. Sorry. Right, going to shower—if the picnic's still on?'

She smiled. 'Oh, yes.'

'Right.' His eyes closed, and his Adam's apple worked furiously for a second. 'OK. Give me two minutes.'

He was at the top of the stairs in three strides, and as she walked through to the kitchen a moment later he crossed the landing wearing nothing more than the water from the shower. Smiling to herself, she retrieved the picnic basket Mrs T had packed from the stone shelf in the larder, where it was keeping cool, and by the time she'd closed the larder door he was back in the kitchen, his jeans yanked up more or less over his hips, his shirt being roughly tucked in as he hopped across the floor putting on his shoes.

'I would have waited,' she said with a smile, and he gave a wry chuckle.

'I just don't want to waste any time,' he said, and, taking the basket from her, ushered her out to the Discovery.

And there, on the passenger seat, was a bunch of willow catkins and hawthorn tied round with a long blade of grass to make a posy.

She picked it up reverently and turned to him, going up on tiptoe and kissing his cheek wordlessly. Then she climbed up into the car, and he slammed the door and went round to his side, sliding in beside her and firing up the engine in one. He dumped the basket on her lap, almost crushing the posy in his haste, and then headed off down the field behind the farm and over the rise towards the river.

'We used to take the tractor—can you remember?' he said with a grin, and she nodded.

'With a flat trailer on the back, and we'd all sit on it and bounce about. We were younger then.'

'Yes.'

Such a world of meaning in one small word. Younger, and free of responsibility and thought and care. They'd had no idea then how fate would take their carefully made plans and turn them on their heads.

In the past, she reminded herself. Live for now.

He was pulling up in the glorious sunshine just beside the willows and alders in their special place. He cut the engine, and they sat for a moment just listening to the beautiful sounds of the day.

Miles away on the other side of the river someone

called their dog, and the spell was broken. Will looked across at her and gave a grim smile.

'You do realise that if we spread that blanket out on the grass, I'm going to make love to you.'

'I'm counting on it,' she said softly.

'It's broad daylight.'

'There's no one here. That person was miles away.'

He swallowed hard, his throat working. 'If I had any sense at all, I wouldn't even take off my seat belt.'

'That would be very uncomfortable,' Izzy said with an impish grin, and he gave a resigned laugh and unclipped it.

'You're a wicked woman.'

'And you love me,' she said, quite without thinking, but he was already getting out of the car and either didn't hear or chose to ignore it, to her great relief.

He took a blanket from the back, told the dog to stay and relieved Izzy of the basket. He spread out the blanket on the soft, sweet spring grass, and set the picnic basket down right in the middle of it, then sat crosslegged on one side.

Hiding a smile, Izzy sat on the other side facing him, and uncovered the basket. 'Goodness knows what's in here; it was your mother's choice.'

'If it's food, it'll be wonderful,' he said, and took a slice of the chicken and bacon tart. 'Dig in. You're going to have to eat loads so she's not offended.'

'Don't. I've already offended her once over this by trying to pay—'

'What? Izzy, you should know her better.'

'I would have gone to the supermarket but I can't drive.'

He shook his head. 'Just eat—but not too much. You can have more later.'

He broke off a piece of the tart and fed it to her, making her lean across and take it with her mouth, and she realised he was looking down her top.

'What is that?' he asked, his voice gruff.

'What?'

'That thing that under other circumstances I might have called a bra.'

She laughed self-consciously. 'It is a bra.'

He shook his head. 'No. It's closely related, by the look of it, to that crazy scrap of nonsense that nearly drove me mad last time, when you made me zip up your jeans. You remember?'

She remembered. 'Close. Same make.'

He groaned and put the slice of tart down. 'To hell with food. Come here. If I don't kiss you I think I'm going to die.'

'I doubt it,' she said, but she went anyway, shifting the basket out of reach and lying down on her back beside him.

'Better,' he said, and then his mouth came down and claimed hers in a fiercely passionate kiss that started as it meant to go on. There was nothing subtle or coaxing about it, just hot and hungry and demanding, and it drove her wild with desire.

'Will?'

'It's OK. I'm sorry. I've just wanted to do that so much.' His fingers were busy sliding up her top, unfastening the front clip of her bra, brushing aside the insubstantial wisp of cleverly cut lace that somehow managed to support her and yet could reduce him to this. How amazing.

His mouth was busy with one breast, his right hand with the other. Then he switched breasts, and his hand was free to roam. He pushed down her jog bottoms and groaned.

'Hell's teeth, they're *worse*,' he muttered gruffly, and dropped a hot, heady kiss on the tiny panel of lace. Then he lifted his head. 'I want you, Izzy,' he said, and his voice was taut, his face expressionless except for the blue fire burning in his eyes. 'I want you like I've never wanted anyone, but we can't do this here.'

Disappointment washed over her, but then common sense followed and she drew him down into her arms, careful not to scrape him with the cast, and cradled his head against hers.

'It's all right,' she said. 'Just hold me.'

He wrapped her against his chest and rolled onto his back, taking her with him. 'If things were different,' he said after a long silence, 'if I didn't have the kids, and you didn't have the press after you everywhere you went, and our lives ever touched—'

He didn't say any more, but he didn't need to. He was telling her yet again that this was all they could have, and she already knew that.

'Shh,' she said, pressing a kiss to the hard, rough angle of his jaw. He'd showered, but he hadn't shaved since the morning, and the slight scrape of stubble on her lips was curiously intoxicating. She kissed him again, trailing her lips over his skin, enjoying the sensation, and he turned his head and captured her lips with his.

This kiss was soft and tender, a gentle unwinding, although she could tell his body was still as taut as a bowstring and raging with need.

'We ought to eat something,' he said after a while, 'and then we should get on. We've got the lambs to check, and I've got a million and one other things to do before I milk Bluebell.'

'You ought to teach me to do it one-handed,' she said with a grin, and he laughed softly.

'You've got quite enough to do in the study—if you can bring yourself to tackle it.'

'I'll tackle it. It won't take long,' she promised, and levered herself up. 'You stay there. I'll feed you.'

He was going to scream with frustration. Her picnic had been a lovely idea, but it had just cranked up the heat another notch and left him even hungrier for the things he couldn't have.

'We're going to have to go back to London,' he said. 'Invent an excuse—you might need the office,' he suggested.

She laughed. 'They all know it's shut. They'd see straight through it.'

'Shopping?'

She gave him a blunt look. 'You, shopping? If I was going shopping, I wouldn't take you. I'd be allowed chainstore white underwear.'

'Don't. It can be very sexy.'

'You think all underwear's sexy,' she said, and he chuckled and turned down the track towards the sheep, glancing as he always did towards Mrs Jenks's cottage.

Funny. He slowed the car and looked again, and sure enough, there was no smoke.

'What is it?'

'Mrs Jenks. She always has the fire lit. Always.'

Izzy shrugged. 'Perhaps she felt it was warm enough.'

He shook his head. 'No. She feels the cold. I think we should check on her.' He turned down her track, and when he reached the end her little dog came running out whining.

'The door's open,' he said. 'I don't like it.'

He headed for the open door at a run, leaving Izzy to follow, and as he went into the kitchen he found the reason for the dog's concern. The old woman was lying back in her chair by the side of the Rayburn, her eyes closed, and for a moment he thought she was dead. Then her eyes fluttered open and she stared at him unfocused.

He crouched down beside her and took her hand. 'Mrs Jenks? It's all right, we're here now.'

'Will?'

He was relieved to hear her voice, but it was thin and reedy, and he knew she was dying. 'Don't talk,' he murmured, squeezing her hand gently.

'Why not? So much to say.' Her fingers tightened on his. 'Thank you for looking after me.'

His throat closed. 'Don't. It's been a pleasure. Let me get Simon or the doctor—'

'No! Not Simon, and the doctor can't help me. I'm dying, Will. Just stay with me. It hurts.'

'What hurts, my love?'

'My heart. It's the end. I know that. I want to die

here, not in some horrible ambulance, bumping along the track with a mask on my face—oohh.'

'Shh. Don't talk now. Just rest. Can I get you anything? A drink?'

'Water.'

Izzy put a glass in his hand. She must have been waiting with it. He held it to her lips, but she only wet them, nothing more.

After a moment she opened her eyes and looked over his shoulder and smiled. 'Izzy,' she said unsteadily. 'You look after him. He's a good man, and you deserve each other after all this time.'

Her eyes closed, and she gripped his fingers for a moment, then looked at him again. 'Is it sunny?'

'Beautiful.'

'I think I'd like to die with the sun on my face,' she said, and gently, as carefully as he could, he lifted her and carried her out into the garden. There was a seat by the back door, and he sat down on it with her cradled on his lap, and she rested her tired white head against his shoulder and sighed.

'That's lovely,' she whispered. 'Thank you.'

Moments later Izzy touched him gently on the arm. 'Will? She's gone.'

'I know,' he said. He felt the tears slide down his cheeks, but he didn't have a free hand to brush them away, and anyway, he reckoned Mrs Jenks had earned them. He stood up and put her carefully down onto the seat, propping her up with cushions that Izzy brought out for him. 'I'll just let her sit here in the sun until they get here.'

He walked away, bracing his arms against the roof

of the car and staring at the ground. Izzy put her arms around him from behind and hugged him gently.

'Are you OK?'

He nodded. 'Yes. Simon will give me hell for not calling him, but he wouldn't have got here. Nor would we—if we'd made love, we wouldn't have been here now, and she would have died alone.'

Izzy released him, and for a moment he thought he'd upset her. Then she opened her side of the car, reached in and brought out the posy he'd made her. Without a word she handed it to him, and he took it and tucked it into Mrs Jenks's hand.

'Thanks,' he said gruffly. Then, and only then, he called the police.

If she thought he'd been busy before, the next two weeks were hell. Simon Jenks wanted to clear out the house immediately, and there were heated discussions about what items of furniture were his and what were not. The executors were involved, and Will was kept running backwards and forwards to the little farmhouse to sort out one dispute after another.

Izzy was feeling much better now, and the pain of her arm was giving way to frustration and discomfort. Still, at least she'd been able to get the office work cleared for him, and his study was now a lovely room with everything in its place.

He was stunned. 'I won't know where to find a thing,' he told her, and she opened the filing cabinet and gave him a quick guided tour of her carefully labelled pockets.

'Good grief,' he said faintly. 'Thank you, Izzy.'

He kissed her—just a quick brush of his lips, but then he hesitated and drew her into his arms, kicking the study door shut behind him and plundering her mouth, threading his strong fingers through her hair and holding her still while he drank from her as if he couldn't help himself.

By the time he lifted his head his chest was heaving and his eyes were dark and smouldering.

'We need to find an excuse to get to London,' she said with a wry, breathless little laugh, and he just rolled his eyes and chuckled grimly.

'I wish. I can't get away from things here long enough to eat at the moment. The chances of a day off are just so remote they aren't worth considering.'

'It'll get better,' she reminded him.

'I'll hold that thought. I have to fly. I've got another meeting with Simon Jenks and the executor—that man will take the wallpaper if I let him. What she did to deserve a son like that I cannot imagine, but God had better have a very good reason.'

'I thought she didn't believe in God?'

'She didn't. She believed in love and human kindness. It's her funeral tomorrow. Will you come with me, Izzy? I don't think I can do it on my own.'

And so, the next day, she found herself standing beside Will during the simple ceremony. Mrs Jenks had elected to have a green burial, and she was laid to rest on the edge of a wood, her simple willow coffin interwoven with flowers from her garden. She knew Will had done that, his last gift to the woman. He held himself firmly in check until the coffin was lowered into the grave.

Then he turned away, and she knew he was thinking of Julia. What could she say to him? How could she comfort him?

She couldn't, but she could take him home. 'Come on,' she said gently, and. slipping her arm through his, she led him to the car. 'I can't drive you, Will. Are you OK to do that?'

He nodded. His eyes were dry, but his face was drawn and haggard and for the first time she understood just how deeply he was grieving for his wife.

She was just a passing diversion, an itch he hadn't finished scratching in his teens. Julia had been his real life, and she was truly deluded if she imagined that she could in any way take the woman's place.

He disappeared the moment they got back to the farm, not even waiting to change but whistling up the dog and striding off across the fields without a word. She let him go. She had no choice, she couldn't have caught up with him if she'd tried, but she didn't want to try.

The funeral breakfast was being held at the Old Crock, courtesy of Mr and Mrs T, and nothing to do with Simon, for all the fuss he'd made—and now it seemed he was contesting the sale of the property, saying she'd been there so long that it still belonged to her and Will had no right to the house. So the café was seething with people who'd genuinely loved the old woman, and she was being given a send-off she would have been proud of.

It was too much for Izzy. The accumulated emotion of the past few days and weeks was getting to her, and the thought of eating anything much was distinctly unappealing. Instead she phoned Emma and arranged to walk over there for lunch. A little exercise and fresh air was exactly what she needed, and she set off over the fields in the opposite direction to Will. There was a track that led down to the village, and she took it, walking out and pushing herself to get her heart pumping and her legs working again after her long period of inactivity.

By the time she reached the village she was regretting it. She felt distinctly light-headed and queasy, because of the lack of food and the heat of the day. It was only early May, but the temperature had soared in the past day or two and it was hotter in the sun than she'd realised.

She knocked on Emma's door and went gratefully into the cool kitchen on the north side of the house.

'You look rough,' Emma said candidly, scanning her face with searching eyes.

Izzy scanned her back and took in the pallor, the circles round her eyes, the hollow cheeks. 'You don't look so great yourself. What's happened, Emma?'

Emma gave a rueful laugh. 'The usual. I'm pregnant again.'

'What? You said you weren't having any more—that three was more than enough—'

'Yes, well, tell it to the fairies. They must have had other ideas. And don't ask me how it happened. I have no idea. We must have made love in our sleep. That's what you get for so many years of harmony. You don't even have to be conscious.'

They laughed, and Emma opened the fridge. 'You need feeding. Fancy helping yourself? If I look at anything more highly flavoured than an ice cube I'll heave.'

But curiously Izzy didn't feel like much either. 'Have you got any fruit?'

'Yeah, sure—in the fruit bowl, or I think there's some melon in the fridge somewhere. And there should be slices of apple in lemon juice and water. When I'm feeling strong I eat them.'

Izzy had a slice of melon and felt better, but sipping iced water and sitting in Emma's lovely cool kitchen were probably also partly responsible. She found herself telling Emma about the funeral, and Will's reaction.

'Poor Will. I wonder if he'll always feel guilty.'

'Guilty?'

'He and Julia weren't always happy. I think he blamed himself. Personally I don't think either of them were to blame. He did his best to be a good husband, and Julia was a dutiful wife and a wonderful mother to those children, but they didn't have any sparkle.'

'But he loved her.' Izzy was sure of that.

'Oh, yes, he loved her,' Emma agreed. 'Just not enough. But that's what you get for "having to get married". Being pregnant is a lousy reason to get married. Do you remember Cathy Bright? Her younger sister got married three years ago because she was pregnant, and they've split up already. She's had another baby, too—trying to patch up their marriage. I often wondered if that's why Will and Julia had Rebecca, but I didn't like to ask, and Julia didn't talk about it very much. She was a very private person.'

How strange. Izzy found it hard to imagine Will and

Julia unhappy. Nothing he'd said had given her any indication of that, and at the graveside today, and again in her roof garden in London, she'd seen real pain in his eyes, the sort of pain that took your breath away.

And besides, he'd told her himself that he loved Julia, eleven years ago, when it had all happened. He'd come to see her, to tell her that he and Julia were getting married, and he'd told her he was in love with her best friend.

Will had never lied to her. She hadn't wanted to believe it, but she'd had no choice. And she had no choice now. Maybe Julia had been unhappy, but it hadn't been for lack of love, of that she was sure.

Emma was in the fridge, raiding the ice cube tray and complaining bitterly about Rob.

'I can't imagine what I saw in him,' she was grumbling. 'I thought he was the sexiest man alive—and look where it's got me! Pregnant for the fourth time, for heaven's sake. It's a good job I love him so much or I'd kill him.'

She sat back down at the table with a handful of ice cubes and offered one to Izzy.

She chuckled and took one, sucking on it while Emma carried on, an ice cube stuck in her cheek while she talked. 'It's knowing it's going to go on for the next few weeks that I can't stand. I mean, I know the routine inside out now. Dizziness, nausea, tiredness—all the time the tiredness, but that might be something to do with all the other kids!—and then the nipples kick in. Sore, tense, prickly—they itch and tingle in the night, and my bra always feels too tight even when it isn't, and then in five minutes or so it will be, and I'll have to go back into my huge bras again for the next few months—oh, I could scream if I had the energy. I loathe it. I loathe Rob. It's all his fault.'

Izzy laughed. There was nothing else to do at such a litany of disaster. 'I'm sorry,' she said, covering her old friend's hand and giving it a squeeze. 'But just think, you'll get a baby out of this. Isn't it worth it?'

Emma snorted. 'Ask me in seven months. No, better still, ask me in ten months. By then it'll be going through the night, if it knows what's good for it, and I might have caught up on some sleep.' She sighed. 'So—tell me about you. How's your arm?'

Izzy looked at it disparagingly. 'Hopeless. It hurts a little still, but mostly it itches and prickles where the wires are. I should have the cast off tomorrow, and it'll hopefully feel better then. I should have gone today, but with the funeral and everything I've had to change the appointment. I'm just hoping Will can take me.'

'Don't bet on it. I heard Rob talking to him on the phone the other night. Simon Jenks is getting right up his nose and I think he's seeing Rob to get all his facts straight about where he stands on the property. Rob doesn't think there's a problem, but he's certainly going to be busy. Want a lift to the hospital?'

Izzy was tempted, but she took one look at her friend's drawn face and shook her head. 'Don't worry, I'll get a taxi. I might go shopping afterwards.'

She didn't go shopping. Instead, once the cast was off and the wires removed—amazingly painless and simple—she took herself off into town, found a beauty salon and begged a manicure. The skin on her arm was horrible, and she needed her nails attended to drastically. The arm was terrifyingly weak, but the girl who did it was very gentle and thorough, and after she was finished Izzy felt more human.

She went back to the farm in a taxi, and she realised when she arrived that she was feeling peckish. She walked into the café, intending to order something light, and the smell of frying bacon hit her in the back of the throat.

She swallowed hard and backed away, turning and running across the yard to the house and only just making it into the bathroom in time. Minutes later, her stomach thoroughly empty and her legs like jelly, she sat down on the edge of the bath, hung her head over the sink and splashed her face with cold water.

It was having the wires removed, she thought. It must have affected her more than she'd realised. She lifted her head and rubbed absently at her breasts with her arm. They were tender. She must have a period due. Thank goodness she'd had the cast off. She'd been wondering how she'd deal with that particular problem one-handed—

She felt the blood drain from her face.

Her cast had been on five weeks. She'd had a period the week before she'd gone to Dublin, just after the party. That had been six weeks ago.

And her cycle was as regular as clockwork. She'd never been a day late in her life.

It must be the shock of seeing Will again, and the fracture, and the change of routine, she told herself. But what routine? She had no routine. Her life was in a constant state of flux.

Which left only one answer.

CHAPTER TEN

SHE couldn't tell Will. Not after what Emma had said yesterday.

Being pregnant is a lousy reason to get married... He loved her—just not enough... I often wondered if that's why Will and Julia had Rebecca... I wonder if he'll always feel guilty—

No. She couldn't tell him. She'd always thought they'd been happy together, and nothing he'd said had given her reason to doubt it. If Julia had been a private person, then so, too, was Will, and she didn't think he'd talk about his marriage.

Although he'd tried to tell her something about Julia before, of course, and she'd stopped him. She'd told him it was in the past, and so it was, but that didn't mean it wasn't still affecting him. Had he been going to tell her that they hadn't been happy?

She worried her lip with her teeth, not knowing what to do and yet knowing that she had to get away. Now her cast was off, although her arm was desperately weak she could use it a little to do things, if she had to, and it would be fine soon, surely?

In direct contrast to her nausea. She'd hardly made it to the bathroom earlier, and if she stayed here any longer Will would cotton on. He'd had two children with Julia, and his mother would start to notice that she wasn't drinking coffee even if Will didn't. It wouldn't take them long to put two and two together, and until she'd got all her ducks in a row she didn't want him knowing about the baby.

Baby.

Her hand went down instinctively to cradle it, her palm lying flat over her taut abdomen. It wouldn't be many more weeks before it started to show, though.

She packed her few things, went round the house gathering together all the little bits and pieces that always seemed to disperse themselves, and then she went out of the back door and round the side, to go across to the café and tell Mrs T she was going, and found herself faced with a barrage of cameras.

Fortunately they were pointing towards the café, but at least it gave her a good excuse for leaving. She hurried back inside, shut herself in the study, pulled down the blind and rang the café. The phone, of course, was engaged, and seconds later there was banging on the front door.

Damn. Was it locked? The back door was never locked, and she couldn't remember locking it just now. She wasn't even sure it had a key. Would they just come in?

She phoned Mr T in the Valley Timber workshop.

'Mr T? It's Izzy. What's going on?'

'Oh, Izzy—you've seen them. I was going to call you. Someone caught sight of you at the funeral yesterday,' he told her, 'and Mrs Willis confirmed your identity, apparently.'

She sighed raggedly. She'd hoped it was nothing to do with her, but that had been too much to expect, and anyway, she needed the smoke screen. 'I need to get away. They won't give up, and I promised Will this wouldn't happen, for the sake of the children.'

'Want a lift?' Thank God he didn't argue.

'I'd love one.'

'Go round the back and wait in the kitchen. Give me a few minutes—and keep out of sight.'

'OK.'

She dragged her things downstairs with her good hand, and lurked in the utility room, bent down behind the freezer, out of line of the window.

The door slammed open and Will came striding in. He caught sight of her and pulled her gently to her feet. His eyes were troubled. 'My father says you're going.'

She nodded. 'I have to, Will. For the kids.'

Emotions chased across his face, but not least was relief, and he didn't try and talk her out it. Quite the opposite. 'I'll take you to the station,' he said firmly.

She shook her head. 'No. It'll just add fuel to the fire, and anyway, I hate public goodbyes. Let your father do it.'

He hesitated, then nodded agreement. 'You're right. Take care, Izzy. I'll miss you.'

He was swallowing hard, and so was she. 'I'll be in touch. Thank you for everything you've done. You've been wonderful.'

God, her heart was breaking, but she wasn't going to cry. She wasn't. She went up on tiptoe and kissed his cheek, and then he handed her bags out to his father and went round to the front to create a diversion while they made their escape over the fields in the Discovery.

Mr T took her to the station and hugged her as he

said goodbye, and there were tears in her eyes then, tears she couldn't hold back.

'Thank Mrs T for me for all her kindness. She's been so good to me. I'll miss her.'

'She'll miss you, too. Don't you be a stranger, now, Izzy. We'll expect you back just the moment this has all settled. You're good for Will. He needs you, and so do the children. They've really taken to you.'

She couldn't speak. Her throat was closed up so tight she thought she'd choke, and she hugged him back hard, then all but pushed him off the train. 'Go on, or you'll be coming to London with me.'

'That'd give them something to talk about,' he said with a wink, and stepped off the train just as the guard blew his whistle and the doors started to slam.

He lifted his hand to wave, but she'd turned away, struggling with tears and the rising nausea that the smell of the train had brought on.

She didn't enjoy the journey.

'So that's that. Simon Jenks hasn't got a leg to stand on with this nonsense. Will? Will, are you paying me any attention?'

Will stared at Rob and scrubbed a hand over his face.

'Sorry. Yes, I'm listening.' In between feeling empty because Izzy was gone and relieved that the press had also gone away.

Still, he'd always known she was going. It had only been a matter of time, and now her cast was off she didn't need them any more. She could wash her hair and dress herself, and shower and all the other things that had been tricky, and for the last few days she'd been looking a bit peaky.

Missing her old life, not unnaturally. She'd be glad to be back, and once he'd talked some sense into himself he'd be glad she was gone.

And he'd do it. Give or take another twelve years.

Izzy was lost. There was nothing to do in London, nowhere to go that she could cope with. Everything either made her feel sick or sad, and above all she was lonely.

She'd never really been lonely before, or if she had, she hadn't really put a name to it. Now, though, she was bereft. Will had only been in her life again for a few short weeks, but the impact had been huge.

Without the baby to think about life would have been unbearable, but now, with this little person slowly developing inside her, the child she'd always longed for in a way she'd never understood, gradually the blackness started to recede and she could see the light again.

And with the dawning of that light she realised that she would have to make some drastic changes in her life.

She was spending all her time in the roof garden, in the shade under the grapevine, sipping iced water and listening to the endless hubbub of the city, longing for the tranquillity of the countryside.

And that was what she'd have to do. She'd move to the country. She would close her business. There was nothing to sell. It was Isabel Inc. Without her it was nothing. She'd terminate her lease, sell on the employment agency and retire to the country with her baby.

The idea held huge appeal, and when Kate rang her and gently broke it to her that she'd met a man in Australia and wouldn't be coming back, she was able to wish her well and genuinely mean it.

'How's that gorgeous man of yours?' Kate asked, and Izzy, who didn't feel up to dealing with Kate's curiosity even long-distance, said he was fine. For all she knew, he was.

He hadn't phoned her, though, and she hadn't rung him. Let sleeping dogs lie. There'd be time. More than enough time. So long as she told him about the baby before it was born, to give him time to get used to the idea, that would be enough.

She was realistic enough to know he'd want to be involved with it, but she wasn't going to give him a chance to bully her into marrying him just to salve his conscience, and so she had to wait until she was strong enough to stand up to him before she told him.

With any luck it would be before the baby went off to university!

She laid a hand on the gentle curve that was their child. 'Where are we going to live, baby? Near your daddy, I suppose. Then you can be friends with Rob and Emma's baby, and Emma will be there for me, and at least I won't be lonely. And your grandparents will spoil you to bits, and you can play with your brother and sister, and it should be a good life. We'll be fine.'

And if she told herself that enough times, maybe it would be true.

She'd have to tell her own parents at some point, as well, but as they didn't approve of her lifestyle, and had chosen to believe a lot of the rubbish that appeared in the press, she felt no need to live near them. They could see their grandchild on carefully edited occasions, and that would be enough. She didn't need their disapproval on a daily basis.

But, of course, she'd need somewhere to live—and to find somewhere she'd need an agent she could trust.

Tom Savage. He'd been at school with them, he'd been at the party at Rob and Emma's, and she knew he dealt in the sort of country property she was looking for.

So she rang him, and told him she was looking for a house close to the village. 'Within, say, five miles?' she suggested, and he promised to call her back. Twenty minutes later the phone rang.

'Izzy. It's Tom. Look, I've got an idea. There's a farmhouse come on the market—it's close to the village, just about three miles south. You might know it. Wildmay Farm. It used to belong to Mrs Jenks.'

Her heart stopped. 'That's Will's,' she said, and he confirmed it.

'He's selling it. The thing is, it needs a great deal of work, but I know money isn't something you're worried about, and it's in the most wonderful spot.'

'I know. I know the house.' She'd been there when Mrs Jenks died. She'd never forget the image of Will sitting there with the dead woman in his arms and tears streaming down his face. 'I'll have to think about it.'

'Well, don't think too long. There's a lot of interest. You might need to move fast. It's got all the barns as well, of course. I don't know why he's selling it; I didn't speak to him for long. He was a bit—short, really. I think he's had a lot of hassle from the son and he just wants to be shot of it.'

Izzy had other ideas, but she wasn't sharing them with Tom Savage. 'Can I buy it anonymously?' she asked. 'Or under a business name?'

'Sure. Can I ask why?'

'Just privacy. I don't want everyone knowing my business.'

'No problem.'

'Good. Tom, we'd better meet. Do you want me to come up?'

'Sure. I can show you round the property if you like.'

'Don't bother. I'll see it later. I don't need to see it before I buy it.'

'In which case, why don't I come to you? I've got to go to the London office on Monday. Why don't we meet for lunch?'

And, of course, as luck would have it, the place he chose was heaving with celebrities and they were spotted by the ever-present paparazzi.

'Oh, damn,' she muttered. 'Why don't you come back to mine for coffee and to do the paperwork? We aren't going to get any peace here.'

'Miss Brooke! Isabel! Is it true that your affair with Will Thompson is over?'

'Is this the new man in your life?'

'Sorry, I'm happily married,' Tom said, and threw a handful of notes at the waiter.

'Excuse me,' she said, as one of the men shoved a microphone under her nose and started asking her more questions about Tom, and he neatly and none too gently deflected him out of her way as he ushered her out of the door. Behind her she could hear camera flashes popping, but they headed out into the sunlight and Tom hailed a taxi, helped her into it and slammed the door behind them.

'Canary Wharf,' he said, and then let out his breath in a rush. 'Are they always like that?'

Izzy laughed. 'Sometimes. Usually they're rude.'

He gave a strangled laugh and ran his finger round his collar. 'How do you cope with it?'

'I don't. That's why I want to buy this place anonymously. I really don't want publicity, Tom.'

He nodded his understanding of the situation, and then pulled out the details again. 'They're only sketchy details as yet, we haven't got the others back from the printer, but they give you information about the barns. I don't know if it's even suitable for you, but it could be a lovely house. Not big, of course, but it used to be two cottages. With a bit of work it could have a sensible layout and there's nothing you'd want to change about the surroundings.'

'Location, location, location,' they said together, and laughed.

'Tom, I'll have it. It's ideally situated for what I want, and I might turn the barns into holiday retreats for stressed executives. You never know, I might end up running it as a bed and breakfast!'

He gave her an odd look. 'I thought you wanted somewhere as a weekend retreat?'

She shook her head. 'No. A lifestyle change. I'm sick of London, sick of my job, sick of being hounded by the press. Hence the secrecy. I want some peace.'

Peace to bring up my child, she added silently.

He nodded. 'I can understand that—but surely, if you're going to be living there, Will's going to know, so what's the point of the anonymity thing on the purchase? It doesn't have to be public knowledge.'

She'd been waiting for that, and she was ready for him. 'I don't want him feeling he's got to let me have it at a good price. I know Will, and he would do something silly like that. If he thinks I'm just another Londoner, with more money than sense, he'll get the going rate, and that's only fair.'

Again, Tom nodded. 'Right. OK, I'll keep it quiet.'

They arrived at her apartment block, but of course the press were there by then and they were photographed going in.

'It would drive me crazy,' Tom said, looking at them over his shoulder as they hurried in.

'It does. Hello, George. Sorry about the fuss outside.'

'No problem, Miss Brooke. I'll get rid of them for you and let you know when the coast is clear.'

'Thank you.'

She took Tom up to her apartment, made him tea and apologised for not having coffee. 'I've run out,' she said, although in fact it was simply that she couldn't yet tolerate the smell. They looked at the paperwork, she contacted her solicitor over the phone and he met them there, and when Tom left two hours later he had an offer thirty per cent over the asking price.

'That's a good margin,' her solicitor said curiously.

'Because I don't want to lose it in a contract race. I want that property, Bill. I intend to have it.'

He nodded. 'Leave it to me. What about the lease on the office? And what about severance packages? Want me to get David Lennox in on this?'

It took days of sorting out, during which the gutter press had a field-day with her 'relationship' with Tom, but finally the business was closed, and the house was secured. All she had to do was sign the papers and transfer the money. She went up in a private car to Tom's office and bumped into Rob, of all people.

'Izzy! How are you?'

'Oh, I'm fine. Just up here to see a friend.'

And then Tom walked out behind her and came over and greeted her, and she could hear the maths going on in Rob's head. Between the fact that Will was selling the little farmhouse, the papers were linking her to Tom and she was standing here in his office, there was plenty to work on.

Rob wasn't stupid—and two and two, in this case, were definitely going to make a lot more than five. However, he didn't stay to air the result of his equation, just smiled briefly and went away, a puzzled frown on his face. She had the feeling she hadn't heard the last of it.

'Damn,' Tom said, and Izzy echoed it a thousand-fold. Of all the people to run into, only Will could have been worse.

'Fancy a look at the house, since you're here?' Tom said after they'd finished their business and put the paperwork away.

She suppressed a little quiver of excitement. She'd been itching to see it, but until now she hadn't liked to. But now it was hers, the money transferred, and Will was unlikely to be there. He would have finished clearing it out ages ago.

And it would have been fine, of course, if he'd hadn't just finished checking the sheep and been heading back to Valley Farm. The cars stopped nose to nose on the track, and Will got out, his face carved from stone, and walked up to her open window. He raked her with expressionless eyes, then looked across at Tom.

'This is private land. I don't want either of you on it.'

She had no idea how Tom was reacting. The shock of Will's words had her reeling, though, and it was a second before she got her composure back. By the time she had, Tom was out of the car and speaking to Will a few feet away.

'The house is sold,' she heard him say. 'The money was transferred to you today.'

'So what the hell are you doing here?'

Tom caught Izzy's eye. 'I'm acting for the new owner.'

'And did you have to bring *her* with you?' He jerked his head at Izzy, and she felt herself recoil from his anger. 'I mean, it's not up to me that you're cheating on your wife, but you don't have to rub my nose in it with the woman I love. Now, get the hell out of here, Tom, before I do something I'll regret, and don't come back.'

The woman I love.

Had he meant to say that? Was it true?

Izzy got out of the car, her legs trembling.

'Tom, you go. I'll talk to Will.'

'I have nothing to say to you.'

'But I have something to say to you, and I'd appreciate an opportunity to say it.'

Tom looked from one to the other, and folded his arms. 'I'm not leaving her with you. You're too angry—'

'He won't hurt me. Not like that, anyway. You go, Tom. Please.'

'Ring me. You've got my mobile number,' he said, and got back into his car reluctantly and backed slowly away, leaving Izzy standing just feet away from the man who, only moments before, had said *the woman I love*.

'Is it true?' she said softly. 'Do you love me, Will?'

He turned to her then, and the pain she'd seen in his eyes before was back in spades. 'I've never stopped loving you,' he said, his voice taut with emotion. 'In all the years I was with Julia, all the time we spent together, always in the centre of my heart was my love for you. And I really, really don't need to see you running around my land with another of my old schoolfriends—'

'I bought the house,' she said, and for a moment he was motionless. Then he lifted his head and stared at her, his face puzzled.

'You?' he said incredulously. 'It was you?'

'Yes. That's why I saw Tom in London, why I'm here today.'

'But—why? A weekend cottage, so you can come up here and jerk my emotions around when it suits you?'

'I've never jerked your emotions around, Will,' she told him flatly. 'It was you that did that to me. You that went travelling the world with my best friend and came back in love with her.'

'No.'

'Oh, yes.'

'No. I told you that because I thought if you hated me it would be easier for you. It's the only lie I've ever told you, Izzy. I didn't love her. I never loved her, not like that. Not in the way she deserved. And I'll regret it for the rest of my life, because she was worth more, but she didn't love me, either, in the end. It took her a while to realise, but then of course it was too late. She was already pregnant.'

'But you'd still had an affair.'

He shook his head. 'No. We slept together once. We were young, we were drunk, and she came on to me. She did it deliberately—said she wanted to know what it was like, just once. But it was enough, and because she was the vicar's daughter, and I'd promised I'd look after her, I had no choice but to marry her—and I've paid for that night over and over again.'

'You've got beautiful children,' she reminded him.

His hard, craggy face softened. 'Yes. I've got beautiful children, and I grew to love Julia and understand her, and she gave me a great deal. I don't regret it, but I regret what I lost, and it's cost me dear. And to see you with Tom—'

'I've told you about Tom and why I was with him.'

His brow creased. 'So why buy the house? If it's not a weekend cottage, then why?'

'Because I wanted to be near you. I've given up my

business. I'm selling my apartment. When the house is done up I'm moving up here.'

'Then why not live with me?'

She laughed unsteadily. 'Because you've never asked me?'

'Because I know I have nothing to offer you—you've got everything, Izzy. I've got nothing.'

'Except my heart.'

She blinked, because she could no longer see him, and then somehow she was in his arms.

'Oh, dear God, Izzy,' he said, and his chest heaved. His trembling hands cradled her face and he stared down at her, wonder dawning in those beautiful, sparkling blue eyes. 'I love you,' he breathed, and then his mouth was on hers, desperate, hungry, then gentling as he folded her in his arms and rocked her against his heart.

'Marry me, Izzy,' he said. 'Be with me. Stay with me. Grow old with me. Have babies, if you want, but for God's sake don't leave me again.'

'Before I say yes, there's something else,' she said, her heart in her mouth. This was so hard. What if he thought she'd done it on purpose?

'Something else?'

'Another reason why I was coming up here to be near you.' She took a steadying breath. 'Will, we're having a baby.'

He stared down at her in confusion. 'But—we can't be. There was only that day in your apartment, and we used something both times.'

She lifted her shoulders in a little shrug. 'I don't know. Maybe there was a fault. The doctor said it sometimes happens. It's rare, but not unheard of—and it's happened to us.'

'So you decided to come back.' His voice was flat.

'No. I decided to leave. And then I decided to come back, because I didn't feel it was fair to you or the child not to be together. I've seen you with your children, Will. You're wonderful with them. I couldn't deny our child that same love, just because we didn't share it, but I couldn't trap you, either. You've been caught like that once. I didn't think it was fair to trap you again. I want you to have the choice, and you still have it. I've bought this house and I can live here, and you can have your child. You don't have to marry me.'

'Oh, yes, I do,' he said. 'I do because I love you, and I've always loved you, and I'm not losing you again. The first time was bad. The second was intolerable. The third time would kill me—so you will marry me, Izzy, if you love me, and you'll let me show you how much I love you.'

'And the baby?'

'Of course I'll love the baby,' he said softly, his hand sliding down between them to rest against her womb. 'How could you doubt it?'

'So what will we do with the house?' she said thoughtfully.

He laughed. 'I don't know. Turn it into a retreat, so we can sneak down here away from the screaming kids and get a bit of one-to-one from time to time?'

She smiled up at him. 'Sounds good,' she said contentedly, but her mind, still tuned to business, refused to switch off. If they were together, she could become properly involved in the running of all the Valley Farm enterprises. While she'd been doing his paperwork, all sorts of strategies had occured to her, but they all needed money—and that she had in abundance. Mrs Jenks's little house and barns were only the start of it, but she didn't bother to tell him her ideas now. There would be plenty of time to discuss it later. Years. For now, she was just enjoying being close to him.

They strolled up the track, arms locked round each other, and when they came to the house he took her hand and led her to the bench outside the door, where he'd held Mrs Jenks in his arms to die.

He sat down and patted his lap, and she curled up against his chest and thought how lucky Mrs Jenks had been, to die like that with the sound of his heart under her ear. Did Will have any idea how much he had to offer?

'You're a good man,' she said softly. 'I love you.'

'I love you, too. I was so sure I'd lost you—even more sure there was no way round it. I never dreamt for a moment you'd give up everything to come up here and be with me.'

'Give up everything? I've given up nothing. You're my everything, Will. You, and our baby, and your children, and your parents, and Rob and Emma and Tom. It's people that matter.'

'There are people in London.'

'Not that I care about. Kate's in Australia, and she's met a man and not coming back. She was my only real friend. This is my home—up here, with all of you. Especially with you.'

He lowered his mouth and kissed her tenderly. 'Then welcome home, my darling,' he said softly. 'Welcome home.'

Sweet Books
Available in July

An Heiress On His Doorstep
Teresa Southwick

Rinaldo's Inherited Bride
Lucy Gordon

Her Stand-In Groom
Jackie Braun

Marriage Material
Ally Blake

The Best Man's Baby
Darcy Maguire

Because of Baby
Donna Clayton

The Daddy's Promise
Shirley Jump

The Boss's Baby Surprise
Lilian Darcy

AVAILABLE FROM

Target • K-Mart • Big W
• selected supermarkets
• bookstores • newsagents

OR

Call Harlequin Mills & Boon
on 1300 659 500 to order
for the cost of a local call.
NZ customers call (09) 837 1553.

Shop on-line at www.eHarlequin.com.au

Join
The Book Of The Month Club
today!

Harlequin's Book Of The Month Club offers you the convenience of receiving your favourite books delivered direct to your door at fantastic prices. Not only do you save money, but you also save your valuable time - don't waste it searching for a parking spot again!

Each month, our editorial staff select the Book Of The Month. Once you join, you will be sent our selection automatically each month - with no postage and handling charge! You will receive great editorial from our best-selling authors, meaning fantastic variety for you. If you prefer, you can return any month's selection, without missing out on any future selections.

A totally flexible way of buying the best stories every month - before they are available in the stores!

What more could you ask for?

☑ Free postage!
☑ Best-selling authors!
☑ Variety every month!

☑ Direct to your door!
☑ Great editorial!
☑ Value for money!

If you would like to sign up or if you have any questions, please call our friendly customer service team on:

Aust: 1300 659 500 NZ: 09 837 1553